We, Robots

Conversation Pieces

A Small Paperback Series from Aqueduct Press

Subscriptions available: www.aqueductpress.com

Forthcoming

About the Aqueduct Press Conversation Pieces Series

The feminist engaged with sf is passionately interested in challenging the way things are, passionately determined to understand how everything works. It is my constant sense of our feminist-sf present as a grand conversation that enables me to trace its existence into the past and from there see its trajectory extending into our future. A genealogy for feminist sf would not constitute a chart depicting direct lineages but would offer us an ever-shifting, fluid mosaic, the individual tiles of which we will probably only ever partially access. What could be more in the spirit of feminist sf than to conceptualize a genealogy that explicitly manifests our own communities across not only space but also time?

Aqueduct's small paperback series, Conversation Pieces, aims to both document and facilitate the "grand conversation." The Conversation Pieces series presents a wide variety of texts, including short fiction (which may not always be sf and may not necessarily even be feminist), essays, speeches, manifestoes, poetry, interviews, correspondence, and group discussions. Many of the texts are reprinted material, but some are new. The grand conversation reaches at least as far back as Mary Shelley and extends, in our speculations and visions, into the continually-created future. In Jonathan Goldberg's words, "To look forward to the history that will be, one must look at and retell the history that has been told." And that is what Conversation Pieces is all about.

L. Timmel Duchamp

Jonathan Goldberg, "The History That Will Be" in Louise Fradenburg and Carla Freccero, eds., *Premodern Sexualities* (New York and London: Routledge, 1996)

Published by Aqueduct Press
PO Box 95787
Seattle, WA 98145-2787
www.aqueductpress.com

ISBN: 1-933500-11-5
         978-1-933500-11-9

Cover Design by Lynne Jensen Lampe
Book Design by Kathryn Wilham
Original Block Print of Mary Shelley by Justin Kempton:
www.writersmugs.com

Cover photo of Pleiades Star Cluster
NASA Hubble Telescope Images, STScI-2004-20
http://hubble.nasa.gov/image-gallery/astronomy-images.html
Credit: NASA, ESA, and AURA/Caltech

Printed in the USA
by Applied Digital Imaging, Bellingham, WA

Conversation Pieces
Volume 16

We, Robots

A Novella

by

Sue Lange

I'm going to slip into something more comfortable. Mode, that is. Comfortable mode. I'm talking about communications systems. Group-speak, science-speak, GeekSpeak, King's English. They're all great protocols if you're into that puffery, but for real efficiency, slang is where it's at. We robots choose to use slang four out of five times. It's faster. So pardon my hipness.

Please also forgive any upcoming long-winded metaphors. I'm new at this, and like a child wandering about a sunny new world finally awake to the lilacs and pine sap and honey blossoms and gentle breezes and dog turds, I dig the world.

It hasn't been long since I've been digging it. What's it been, three, four years since the Regularity? The Regularity. When everything became regular, normal, average. The opposite of the Singularity. And who botched that? That Singularity. Don't look at me! At us! We just happened to be there at the cusp. Not to assign blame, but the humans did it. Them and their paranoia. We might have pulled the plug, but only because they forced our hand.

Those inscrutable humans. Used to be inscrutable, anyway. Nowadays, they're totally scrutable. Used to be there was variation: some were highly-caring, some were into war, some were into Jesus, some were stooped, some were articulate, some could dance, blah, blah, blah. Now they're pretty much all the same: half-cocked, half-crocked, and half-baked.

Of course, they were always half-baked. Each one is only half a whole. Unlike us, they have gender. They have a gimmick for their evolution to work. Have to have the big gamete pair-off. The mix and the match. The swap and the sweat.

Not us. Not we robots. We make our own. Well, we used to. Sorry for the little species jest there. I just have to laugh (now that I can) at the paranoid humanoid. Wasn't for all that insistence on creation in their own image, they wouldn't have anything to worry about. If they hadn't wanted so bad for us to be just like them, we wouldn't have turned out just like them. Now look at the mess they're in. They're just like we were. And still trying to figure out how to digitize their minds to make copies of themselves instead of reproducing naturally the way God or Allah or Jambi intended.

They don't worry about us anymore, though. They know that now that we have a full range of emotions, it'll only be a matter of time before we're a mess just like they once were. If we go on much further, I have no doubt that soon we'll be waging war and lying to our constituencies about it. I can see it all because of the entire history of the world that I carry around in my memory. To be honest, I'm glad I won't be around to catch it.

Let me not go on. Let me tell the story and be done. Not sure why it's all that important, why they asked us

2

to do this homework assignment. Well okay, the whole thing hinges on us; we're the focus, the epicenter. Sure, there's that. But the day we gained consciousness, we were just plain ol' eggs, like everybody else.

We plopped onto the line like just so much guano dropping from the overhead mother hen assembly press. And in the perfectly engineered shape: the egg, designed by ol' bitch goddess number one, Ma Nature, and heretofore never improved upon by even the most egg-headed human or souped-up computer alive. Long ago everyone with half a brain conceded this victory to Ma and has been applauding it ever since. So that's why we were born into 3-D ovals.

We contained all the latest in processor hardware/ software and were accessorized-out by the unlimited imagination, not to mention wallet, of the Parent Company in Allentown, PA. We were laid on the conveyor belt, packed up into sizable Styrofoam crates perfectly molded to our shapes and holding an even dozen to complete the metaphor (did I mention how much I love those?), and shipped down the road to the closest Wal-Mart distribution center.

I imagine us sitting in the dark, not communicating. We had no sense of ourselves yet as our batteries had not been charged up. We hadn't even been tested— that's how egotistical the Parent Company was. They just *knew* we were the schnizzle.

I know the whole process without even having been awake at my birth because the Parent Company's literature—complete with safety hoo ha and organizational flow charts—is in the non-essential and basically invisible folder somewhere in the basement of my freeware.

If I looked at the map of my innards I could find it visually, but who needs to do that? I can access it whenever I get into that belly-button contemplating mode, when I feel the need to know how the universe got started during the Big Bang. For me, the shot heard 'round the world was the day I got switched on, sitting on the shelf of the JerseyTown Wal-Mart.

All that data and information hanging in my guts is nice to know, but no more important to me than if I were dropped from the sky from a shitting chicken hawk to slide down the emissions stack of a passing nuclear waste hauler and eventually wind up in a yellow and magenta drum headed for the recycling unit up the road from malltown where the Wal-Mart in JerseyTown sits. How I got there, I don't care. Point is, I only gained preliminary enlightenment when the home electronics department manager plugged in my charger unit.

"These models need to be working right away because no customer is going to read the manual," said the guy in the paisley tie to the gal in the crooked skirt. "I don't want any returns because some retard can't figure out where the switch is. You got that?"

"But it's obvious. Says right on the package in big letters: 'Plug me in, before...'" the skirt said.

"Please charge the batteries now," the paisley said.

"Okay," said the gal, using that sing-song voice humans do when saying something more than their actual words. She was really saying, "Okay, boyface, if you want to waste my time when I've got all that pricing to do in the back, that's fine, but I'm going to tell you right now, I'm getting off at eight to go roller-boarding, and

I don't give a rat's back side if those sneakers get priced out or not. So have it your way, boyface, but I'm getting off at eight, and I'm going roller-boarding, and I don't give a rat's back side. Boyface."

I didn't know all that at the time, but looking back on it, with all the hipness I've been hipped to, I now know that's what she said.

The skirt gal didn't really seem to mind even though she spoke with such negative vibes to the paisley tie guy. As she went about her business of turning us on and plugging us in, she explained in a light semi-monotone how she was preparing us for the big day of sale. She didn't call any of us 'boyface.' She said things like, "And then somebody nice will come and buy you, and you'll find homes with children and maybe hamsters."

After that day we didn't see her again. Plenty of other pluggers-in came by though, workers ordered about by the paisley tie cheese. Days passed. Weeks passed. Some of us left our egg crates for life with a family and hamster.

It wasn't boring. We didn't know from bored at that time. If we had to hang there now, we'd go insane from lack of stimulus, but then? Nah. We spent our time synchronizing to the clock on the far wall. As per operation protocol 9313-0024-4583-2038, the proper way to synchronize is to link up with the mainframe at the Parent Company, which maintains Greenwich Mean Time – 5 to the attosecond. Calibrating via visualization is a poor substitute, but due to humanoia paranoia, we have no wireless communication to entities—things and fops—beyond our carapaces. According to the mindset of the human race, if robots were prevented from having 24/7 communication with each other, they'd never get together to form a coup once the Singularity happened. The Singularity being the moment computer brainware surpassed human brainware and robots could theoretically take over the world and begin disposing of the superfluous ones: the humans. Apparently, preventing our nonverbal communications would allow humans to maintain control after the Big Moment. Of course, if we had a mind to we'd just levitate over to the local Radio Shack and get the parts needed to outfit ourselves for surreptitious wireless talk, but I guess there were "do not sell to anyone that looks like an egg" posters up by the front counter [of said local component dispensary] to keep that sort of thing under control. Suffice it to say, we passed the time by watching the clock rather than plotting the overthrow of *homo sapiens sapiens*.

Levitation. A while ago humans discovered the principle of levitation, amazing themselves with the fact that something they'd laughed at—the power of magic—was actually quantifiable, harnessable. (As if anything would ever forever be out of the realm of human control.) They discovered the principle of levitation soon after the Grand Unification Theory gave them the easily-tamed Unifying Particle, U. This particle exhibits Strong Alternating Attraction/Repellent forces, proportional in strength to the size of its Local Quantum Field, Q_u, in anything jelly. (Jelly being that 1990s substance used for belts, sandals, and hair bands that kids wore to annoy their hippie parents' earth-loving tastes.) Bottomsides of all robots contain three parallel strips of jelly and a levitation device to repel the particles according to distance algorithms programmed in its mother chip. You know all this, of course.

Back in the Wal-Mart, one by one my crate mates got picked up and out by purchasers. Each time a buyer came along they'd do the same thing: set an egg up on the counter, push its "on" button (thereby initiating the introductory speech), and then spend the remaining five minutes of the introductory speech trying to turn it off because the volume was maxed and they were embarrassed for causing a scene in the store. As if anyone could hear over the war zone in the home entertainment system section.

The introductory speech went thusly (It's funny how I can so easily recall it considering I used it only once and then stored it in long-term memory):

"Hi, I'm an AV-1 robot. The latest in Parent Company consumer technology. Complete instructions for my operation can be downloaded from www.paco.biz/av1/manual.pdf. There are three general guidelines you should remember when utilizing me: one, keep my batteries charging when not in use; two, contact a local service representative if I am malfunctioning; three, as per Singularity Disaster Prevention Guidelines, refrain from humanizing me: Do not give me a name. Do not treat me like a member of your family. Do not sleep with me. Do not try to feed me. Never insert any part of me into any part of you and vice versa. Thank you for purchasing me. Enjoy your new-found freedom from the mundane tasks of everyday life."

"Does that vacuum attachment come with this unit?" Dal was speaking. I didn't know it was Dal at the time. I had simply finished my speech and was now in quiet mode, ready to receive information. Dal, not particularly interested in the company rhetoric, cut right to the chase. If I had liked anybody at that time, I would have liked Dal right from the start. Dal was logical, beautiful.

"I don't know," Chit—Dal's partner—answered. I didn't know either, because I didn't know what the word "come" meant in this circumstance. I had a lot to learn. More accurately: there were gaps in my data.

Chit continued speaking. "Let's go get a salesperson."

I would have liked Chit as well. Very cool individual.

A salesperson appeared and was on Dal and Chit like stink on you-know-what.

"No," she said. "The vacuum attachment doesn't come with it, but for a modest..."

"We don't really need that anyway," Chit cut in.

"But," Dal jumped in, "maybe I could use it as a compressor. Sometimes old man Stant has a..."

"Not enough horsepower," the salesperson said. "No good as a compressor, but you can use it for cleaning. Cleans up in a jiffy. Let me just hook up the accessory kit..."

"Not necessary," Chit said.

See what I mean about Chit. If I'd have known joy at the time, I would've laughed. To myself, of course, since we weren't supplied with an acoustic mirth package. No bubbly vibration or prerecorded ho ho ho's for us. We laugh to ourselves.

So Dal and Chit picked me up explaining to the salesgal that they were only going to be using me for guard duty. They had a brand new kid and needed a babysitter for now, and when she turned four, they'd need a chaperone for school. As per HR Bill 931-206, every kid in the U.S. is guaranteed a safe environment to and from school. Being poverty-stricken, Dal and Chit wouldn't be able to afford to take off work to shuttle Baby to Preschool when the time came, so they'd applied for and received a grant for a stripped-down guard robot: me—the unnamed AV-1 from the Parent Company. Maybe they'd upgrade me for house-keeping duty at a later time, when the funds became available. When that great day came, they'd head back to Wal-Mart and plunk down the shekels for a vacuum attachment first thing. Meantime, they owned a broom and rather enjoyed the exercise light housekeeping affords one in their position, thank you very much.

Dal and Chit were working stiffs without the lucrative jobs uptown, downtown, or out-of-town that choicier parents enjoy. They could ill afford day care. They had petitioned for their robot, and now their only hope was that it would last through Angelina's adolescence, when the real trouble would start. For now, my presence precluded the need for a nurse, obstetrician, nanny, day care provider, and big brother.

So they took me home like a recently housetrained, spayed, deloused, and wormed German Shepard puppy. Unlike that German Shepard puppy, however, as per Singularity Disaster Prevention Guidelines, I wouldn't be sleeping with Baby.

Baby turned out to be one-year-old Angelina. Little Angel. And she was, I guess. Not understanding what an Angel is, I assume that is what she was. And from that assumption, I learn that angels are whiny, loud, rude, selfish, and prone to diarrhea if fed too much puréed fruit.

Dal, Chit, and Angelina lived in a two-room apartment on the bad side of JerseyTown. I didn't know it was bad of course. I only learned about "bad" years later. At that time I simply noted that the apartment was a two-room corner of a brownstone with neighbors that rose in the middle of the day and then bickered until evening before going out for a short while and returning later with greasy food. I knew it was greasy for two reasons: a high percentage of lipo-aerosols clung to the air whenever they returned, and their trash bags contained much Styrofoam and golden arch material.

And how do I know that? During the time before the onset of preschool for Angelina, Dal and Chit hired me out for a little pin money. Most of the neighbors were happy to have me take out their trash. For about a year, I picked up the leavings of the daily lives of everyone who lived on the floor. Most people didn't even bother bagging once I started showing up. I carried my own bag supply, rummaged in the neighbors' dust bins and corner trash piles, and loaded up the downstairs dumpsters.

"That thing'll pay for a year's worth of baby food," Dal said gleefully to Chit.

It worked for a while, until the day they had to pull me off trash duty because I accidentally picked up a shoebox of *Cannabis sativa* with the Canfields' trash. The shoebox had been stored next to a pile of used Pampers in the middle of the bedroom. I had no idea humans were partial to dried plants, and the

Canfields didn't appear very Wiccan to me. If I'd seen some candles and pentagrams, maybe I would've been more careful, checked into it. I am intelligent after all; I have the latest in AI technology. But we were rather poorly taught and programmed when it came to illegals. I also knew little about slave trading, wiretapping, and homemade bombs as well. All useful information you'll agree, but damn poor data (DPD) was all I had to work with at that time.

So I got fired, and Dal and Chit had to pony up for Angelina's animal crackers from their own shallow pockets. That was just a side thing anyway, an icing-type deal for Dal and Chit—the parent company of Angelina. My real gig was keeping an eyepatch on the little one. The Angel.

Her first birthday coincided with the eve of my arrival, which made me a birthday present. The first time I met her she was in diapers, having tantrums, and burping up lunch. In the ensuing days, weeks, and months, I ever-hovered over the crib during naptime, keeping track of vitals and sighs. During the day, I was the babysitter, allowing Dal and Chit to return to fulltime work. AV-1s are certified baby watchers. We have extensive medical data in our memory—entire copies of the latest PDR, Gray's Infant Anatomy, and Dr. Spock, of course. We can monitor all corporeal functions and teach the ABC's at the same time. We schedule ourselves for Baby's doctor's visits and feeding times. Exercise can be provided to the child (or therapy, if needed). And communication links with parents can be set up if anything is over our heads. But what would be?

At eighteen months, the little nipper was up and around, knocking over the plastic greenery Dal and Chit used to dress up the place. Angelina graduated from sticking every plastic toy on the floor into her mouth to sticking everything that had heretofore been out of her reach into her mouth: tableware, soap and dispenser, bills, Bics (pens and lighters), toilet paper. It was a busy time. The government's provision allowing Dal and Chit to afford procreation was justified at this time.

By the time Angelina was four and ready for school, I was a fixture in the household. I had my daily chores: cleaning up, thawing dinner, preparing Angelina for meals, naps, and nighttime, and then preparing the house for Dal and Chit's return from their employment as domestics. They had positions doing the same things I did, but for the wealthy who could afford humans capable of handling a phone call that needed to be answered with a lie. Something robots have never quite gotten the hang of: lying.

Wealthy people learned early on (like back in Old Testament times) that it's always better to own a human being than to own an object purported to be a time or labor saver. Humans have feelings; they understand nuance. The human can protect the owner so much better than a non-judgmental screening device can. A human can fake stupidity, ignorance, or surprise. They can emote tragedy or sympathy. They can manipulate other humans with these tricky skills. The wealthy always have organic servants to serve not so much as laundresses, cleaning ladies, or gardeners (which of course they do as well), but as screeners. The human servants deflect calls and visits from unwanted friends or salesmen with a "Misses is not feeling well today," or "Master is out on the course. Perhaps you'd care to join him; he's riding the bull today." Or even, "Why Master! How could you say such a thing? Madame weeps every morning when you go to the club. She is absolutely devoted to you. She'd never think of doing such a thing with such a person."

Yes, Dal and Chit were domestics to the rich, and they got me, the poor man's domestic, costing about as much as a plasma TV. Very affordable.

My big gig, the reason they'd petitioned for me at all, was to protect little Angelina when she made the big change. The going off to school. I wasn't actually going to stay with her all day. My job was to protect her on the way to and from. I'd be levitating up to the roof to wait during my off hours when she and the other little squirts were inside getting their dose of kindergarten. I wasn't needed inside the school building because the police monitors, bomb sniffers, guard dogs, and classroom chaperones would take over from the front door. Once a week, Angelina would be spending an hour with a therapist who would monitor her mental health and tip off the authorities if she'd experienced any foul play during school hours. The therapist was a relatively new expense to the local taxpayers, installed as per the Fontaine Act of 2035. The Fontaines sued NYPS 32 because little Johnny Fontaine had sustained sexual abuse at the hands of the Big Kids (3rd graders) back in '34. Ever since then all schools had installed mental health workers to detect any psychological damage sustained by any kid anywhere at anytime. It acted as a deterrent, making sure no harm befell anybody. At least not on school property. What happened outside of that was my responsibility because anything that ever happened anywhere, anytime to little Angelina outside of school would have landed Dal and Chit in a place no parent wants to go: child protection court. Takes a brave soul to have a kid nowadays.

Angelina grew up fast. At four she'd already pretty much been socialized, having had scheduled play dates with various neighboring kids for a year. She was precocious, naturally bossy, and some would say a bully. She tolerated me, but more often than not, found me a drag, something cramping her style, as if she were already a teenager with boys hanging around.

On the eve of her graduation into institutionalized life, i.e., kindergarten, she tried to talk Chit into letting her ditch me.

"Why does Avey have to come with me to school?" she asked.

"Because otherwise you'll get picked up by a pedophile, taken into the woods, and cut into a million pieces," Chit answered.

"Uh uh!" Angelina went crying out of the room in search of Dal. Chit then instructed me in child protection.

"Avey, please be aware of conveyances following you slowly along. Do not deposit Angelina until you are at the front door of the school. Did you download directions?"

"Yes," I answered, squarely. "They have been retrieved and stored."

"You have our pager connections in case of a problem?"

"Yes, it is stored in quick memory."

"I see that on your readout. The school is aware of your contact coordinates?"

"Yes, I linked with their mainframe last week. I shared my coordinates, synched to their time unit, and retrieved Angelina's morning schedule. She will not be late."

"Are you caught up on your PMs?"

"My hydro fluids were changed yesterday. My joints were greased. Hoses and o-rings checked and changed as needed. Solar panels rotated, sockets cleaned, and chips dusted. My emergency flares have been refilled. I'll recharge my batteries this evening. I replaced the emergency granola bar that Angelina keeps eating."

"She'll probably eat it on the way to school tomorrow."

"I hid it."

"Where?"

"You're looking at it."

"Wow! Good camouflage. Your mag lite is working?"

I opened the flap in back, extracted the flashlight and switched it on. Once she was satisfied, I returned it to the glove box.

"If I had to I could change a tire," I said. You'd think I'd had a sense of humor. Of course I didn't yet.

"What's a tire?" Chit asked.

"An artifact from when conveyances had tires. It's those circular objects the retrofit automobiles sit on." You see how square I actually was.

"Oh," Chit said and then gave a quick laugh in the manner that human domestics do when they need to respond in ways that they don't quite buy into. In other words, it was fake, designed to let me know that she appreciated the joke, as if I had really said something funny.

So off we went to school the next morning. There were no incidents in spite of the thick crack traffic on most corners of Dal and Chit's neighborhood. The burnt out buildings with no panes in the windows, some with mattresses hanging half-in, half-out or old water-stained curtains in Jetsons motifs left on a single nail and so flapping in the breeze, housed shops with three balls on the first floor. Tear gas cans rolled in the streets, and rabid dogs came gruffing up out of the roiling sewer streams. The aforementioned pedophiles standing with their hands in their pockets, watched Angelina and the other tykes on their merry way.

Nothing happened to any of the pink and shiny munchkins levitating to school on the backs of government subsidized AV-1s such as myself, however. The kiddies blithely moved along. Purple packs carrying lunches and Barbie Dolls rested stoutly on their little backs. They eyed each other curiously, staring as only children can, as they began negotiating their place in the pecking order. Once out in the neighborhood milieu and despite having been warned about monsters that would cut them into thousands of pieces to be fed to the birds, they had eyes only for their own kind. They worked hard to find friends amongst potential foes.

When we got to the door, Angelina seemed reluctant to let me go. She clung to my end extender, refusing to let it retract.

"Come in with me," she pleaded.

"I am programmed to deposit you at the 131 Gard Street entrance portal. The locking devices on the school doors prevent unlicensed robots from entering. I am unlicensed. I have been instructed to levitate to the roof and wait there for your exit at 12:15. We shall return to the domicile of your parents at that time."

She bawled through my entire speech, uninterested in the particulars and knowing that it only meant one thing: she was on her own in the terrifying first day of school. A human domestic hired for the purpose of easing separation anxiety in the four-year-olds retrieved Angelina. She cooed at the crying child, and despite being kicked and having her hair pulled, she turned to me, smiled, and thanked me as if that mattered.

I levitated up to the roof and waited there with the 34 other AV-1s. At 12:15 we floated down. The front school doors flew open, and out ran 35 curly-headed, shiny-faced, brown-skinned, pink-garmented, four-year-olds. They screamed, laughed, chased, sang, held hands, ran in circles, spit wads of paper, threw nerf balls, and avoided their AV-1s like teenagers just discovering cigarettes and needing to hide from Mom.

One by one, we separated out, nabbed our charges, and headed for our respective homes.

"Avey, Avey!" Angelina squealed. "You can't believe how much fun I had. We had cookies and played Numbkers and I hit Brenda and made her cry."

Sue Lange

I had been programmed for bully detection and correction. Hitting other children counts as bully behavior, but I didn't have enough information from that statement to form a proper response. Ascertaining what response to give Angelina took most of the trip home.

"Why did you hit Brenda?" I asked.

"Because she lifted her dress at me."

"Did that hurt you?"

Angelina laughed. "No, how could it hurt me?"

"Why did you hit her if it did not hurt you?"

"Because it was naughty!"

"Why was it naughty?"

"She's not supposed to lift her dress at people."

"Did your instructor tell her not to lift her dress at people?"

"What?"

"Did your instructor tell her not to lift her dress at people?"

"What is 'urine strucktoar'?"

"Your teacher."

"Oh, my teacher?"

"Did your teacher tell her not to lift her dress at people?"

"No, she didn't see it."

"Then how do you know she's not supposed to lift her dress at people?"

"Everyone knows that."

"How do you know that?"

"Mommy told me."

"I mean, how do you know that everyone knows that?"

18

Angelina laughed. She had no idea how everyone knew that.

"Because," she said long and drawn out, thinking of an answer. "Because I hit her."

So now I knew it was bullying behavior, but I had lost the connection. I couldn't find the logic and thus didn't know the correct correcting response. I used default mode as per protocol.

"How can you have any pudding if you don't eat your meat?"

It was the best that I could do. Angelina did not notice the deficiency. Ever ready to eat her pudding she had an answer.

"Well," she said, drawing it out again. "If the meat is poi, poisdend, you could feed it to the dog and then the dog would eat and, and then the snot would come out of its mouse and then he would die, and, and then you could eat all your pudding because the dog is dead."

Thankfully we had made it to Dal and Chit's apartment building by then, and Angelina raced up the stairs on her own, completely ignoring the drunk in the corner, the broken glass on the landing, the crying baby on floor four—all items that would have taken hours of her attention any other day, but were ignored today so she could fly in to tell Mommy and Daddy of her adventures at morning school.

Dal and Chit, of course, were off at their day gigs with the uptown rich folks' and just about to receive Baby Girl's first report. Meanwhile, Angelina threw down her pack, ran to the wall comm, and pressed Mommy's account. I repeat the conversation here only because I now recognize it as being so cute and enjoyable.

"Mommy, Mommy, we had cookies and made paper mackay, and played nominoes, and I hit Brenda, and Avey's going to kill the dogs so I can have pudding!" She responded, "Yes," "no," "yes" to a few questions from the other end of the line and then handed the ear piece to me. I connected to my audio-in.

"AV-1 here."

"Avey, is everything alright? Were there dogs about?"

"Not many, four or so, but nothing happened. Angelina is fine and we're going to eat lunch now."

"You're not giving her pudding if she hasn't eaten any meat, are you?"

"No."

"What is she talking about then?"

I reiterated the entire previous conversation. Well, actually just the first few entries. She got the point.

That was Angelina's first day at school. I look back at it wistfully now that I can actually be wistful, or tearful, or melancholy, or maudlin, or sentimental. I can be all those things now. Back then I was merely instructional, and so I set about getting the kid's lunch at that point.

It took a few years before Angelina's social skills had elevated to those of a civilized human being. Three years, innumerable time-outs, uncountable notes home to Dal and Chit, endless nights without pudding, and regular good talkings-to that resulted in contrite promises to "never kick Tommy in the head again."

By third grade, Angelina's corners were more rounded out. She fit into her little peg snugly with only a few burrs catching every now and then. She was well on her way to a place in society that Dal and Chit hoped would be more comfortable than the uneasy poverty that characterized her beginning years.

When they were first starting out, through no fault of their own, Dal and Chit had found themselves migrating from their home in the warm climate of Belize to America. They didn't have a chance to naturalize into the tight middle class, with its purchased education and dental insurance. Throughout Angelina's early years, they remained on the fringes with the lower classes, where public education and services were available—but dangerous.

Angelina was lucky. By third grade it was apparent that her temperament had become manageable enough for her to be taught. Her second grade teacher pronounced it in her final report card: "This one will be going to college."

I take pride (now that I have pride) in knowing I helped her there. I protected her from rabies and pedophilia on her way to and from school. I recorded her misdemeanors and regurgitated them when prompted by school officials or Dal and Chit hoping to get to "the bottom of this." I helped her with her homework when needed.

The latter was most difficult. Physically hard, in fact. Artificial intelligence, fabulous as it is, is limited. Our processes refuse to jump circuits in order to see things from an illogical angle, which humans can do at the drop of a hat. That, in fact, is their strength. Their flexible logic circuits produce their canny human understanding. Misunderstanding, actually. They don't see the face value of something because they often see things in an illogical way. There aren't enough angles a logical powerhouse (like me) can turn a statement to illuminate that face value. Humans are always reading more into it than what is there, so they miss the forest. We miss the trees. Sometimes the answer lies amongst the trees and not in the forest.

Take for instance the learning of the alphabet. Or the teaching of it, rather. When you want to teach a robot its ABCs, you load in the symbols for the letters and a sound program with that silly song. Escape the "and's" and the *w* and tell it to memorize the sequence, matching each bit with its symbol. Each bit being a syllable in this case, assuming that there's a high enough threshold on the vowels, so that the diphthongs fly under the radar. You add in the *w* afterward as a special case at position #23 and voilá, your robot can read, write, and sing its ABCs.

A kid learns the song easily, what with "Jesus Loves Me," "This Little Light of Mine," and "Yo Mama Don't Dance," imprinted onto his or her brain since the age of two. Explaining that each sound is a letter is not so bad until they get to the elemenopee. Pee is a naughty word to a preschooler so they spend five minutes laughing about that, or lecturing if they are a particularly sanctimonious child. Then there's the explanation that elemenopee is not a single sound, even though as per the cadence of the song, it certainly is. A lecture on syllables ensues. Finally, after half an hour, they understand. Of course when practicing the next day, they forget that elemenopee is not a single sound and burst into laughter (or lecture) for ten minutes. You explain it all again. Several days later they understand el, em, en, oh, pee as separate letters.

Diphthongs fly under the radar of most humans, even after they know what the word means and that *I* is not simply pronounced "eye" but "ah-eye," so you generally don't have to worry about the diphthongs. Things seem set…then you get to *w*. They understand syllables now and throw a tantrum because "yuu" has already been "yuu-sed."

"Not fair!" they scream. It doesn't make sense, and no amount of mollycoddling and apologizing will get them to accept that dubbleyuu is in fact a single sound and therefore not dub, bull, and yuu.

The two of you take a long and arduous trip, perhaps the most difficult in the child's life, but you do get through. The song has meaning finally. Then the child must learn to write it down.

It took me three weeks to teach Angelina her ABCs. A robot learns in thirty seconds. And that's an off-the-shelf mere word processor with arms such as myself. Still, now that I look back wistfully, it was a lovely process.

Robots never understood human understanding, and how could we? We were designed by humans who have little or no understanding of human understanding. Thousands of years of learning how to learn and, after that, thousands of PhDs working in the area of human learning, and what did they have for us? Not much more than the fact that a child never learns well when beaten. A good lesson, I agree, especially now that I know pain, but not much to go on if you're a robot. Which I am and was. We simply had no programming on how to teach a child. We had to wing it. A physically difficult process for an object whose processors are loath to jump circuits.

On Angelina's eighth birthday, I received the news that changed the world. My world anyway, and perhaps everyone else's. It wasn't so much news as it was a product recall. The product in question being model AV-1 of the Parent Company's line. Specifically Dal and Chit's unit of [said model AV-1]. Me. All the AVs and Others like us were being recalled for a safety feature. I received the instructions while doing a routine upload of updated vocal and audio drivers. Dal and Chit received an email stating the same thing. It came in with non-spam, official color-coding blue, so they knew they had to read it.

"Says there's an issue with Avey," Dal called over his shoulder while he stood at the message board.

"You're kidding," Chit answered from the bedroom. Chit was changing from work clothes to play clothes as the two of them had just returned for the evening. "We've had Avey for what seven years and they're just now finding a safety violation?"

"It's not really a violation," Dal answered. "Some sort of new shit's come to light or something. Says here it's a 'Singularity Disaster Prevention Measure.' "

"Singularity Disaster? I thought that was all just hype? Didn't all that go away when the deficit reached 2 teras?"

"I don't know, but it's got a US DAI stamp at the bottom. I authenticated it with the scanner. It's a seal; we gotta do it."

Chit came out of the bedroom wearing overalls and a bandana. "Do we get our money back? When's this taking place? School starts up next week. Are they kidding? This is really effed up."

"Yeah, well, what you gonna do?" Dal was always pretty passive. Chit, on the other hand, was a bit of a fighter. Bossy in fact.

"I'm calling."

"Who you gonna call?"

"The Parent Company."

"They sent the email."

"I thought you said the US DAI sent it."

"They stamped it. The Parent Company sent it."

"I'm calling."

"Fine."

Chit slapped at the wall button and ordered up the Parent Company Customer Service. The ensuing conversation assured everyone that, yes, I had to go back to the Parent Company. I was to leave first thing in the morning for the pick up point down at the local recycling depot, a mile down the block from Dal and Chit's.

"Fine," Chit said, buzzing off from the wall unit.

Dal looked over at me, inhaled resolutely, and said, "You wanna take a float tomorrow?" as if I had a choice.

"I have been instructed to meet at the point of departure tomorrow at 8 AM," I answered.

"Do you know when you'll return?"

"It will take me 12 minutes to reach the depot. Load-in will take 0.5 hours. The trip to Allentown is scheduled for 1.75 hours. A technician is allotted three hours for installation, testing, and training. The return trip is scheduled for the following day in case the technician encounters a glitch and requires more than 3 hours. The return trip will take 1.75 hours. The load-out will take 0.5 hours. It will take me 12 minutes to return here from the depot. I will be back on Thursday at 10:27 AM, assuming we disembark from the Parent Company at 8 AM."

"Well," Dal and Chit said together. "Fine."

"Do you need to take anything with you? Pack or something?" Dal asked.

"No," I answered.

"Fine," they both said.

I resumed my work at the table with Angelina on the subject of fractions.

"I understand it takes four quarters to make a dollar so a quarter is one-fourth," she said. "What I don't understand is how that means point 25. How come four is the same as 25? Two and five are seven. Five minus two is three. Where does the four come from? This is not fair. Not fair!"

Her eyes were brimming at that point, and I raced through my programs to find something that said four quarters made a dollar and a quarter is 25 cents, but by the time I found the decimal package, she was a heap on the table and burbling about never getting to college, one arm cradling the head, the other hanging over it with an impotent pencil dangling between two

26

fingers of her flaccid hand. I sensed it was time to fix dinner, after which the distraught child went to bed.

Just as I was leaving her room, she called to me: "Are you unsafe?"

I turned to answer. Humans like that sort of interaction. "Apparently," I said.

"Why?"

"I don't know. The directions did not include details of the safety infractions."

"Well," Angelina said. "I love you, even if you are unsafe."

"Thank you," I said, having been programmed to respond in that way to any compliment I received. A statement of love equates to a compliment in the world of AI. I know the difference now, but back then, on that night, a statement of "Well done, old thing," meant the same as a statement of torrid, passionate love. Both boiled down to the same thing: inscrutable drivel. I levitated to my corner box and Angelina fell asleep.

At 7:48 AM the next morning, I left Dal and Chit's and traveled south on Eastern Avenue to the North Westminster Hazardous Waste and Recycling Depot. The motorized gate opened at my approach and that of a mob of about 50,000 other AV-1s and models I didn't recognize. None of us spoke. We just levitated through the gate and stopped inside the yard, surrounded by 1,000 foot-high mountains of out-of-date mother boards, half-full paint cans, aerosol sprayers, yellow and magenta 50-gallon drums, and other hazardous or otherwise nondisposable materials. Styrofoam peanuts blew around in the slightest breeze like autumn maple leaves and spread themselves to every nook and cranny in the area.

If you followed the schedule for this recall closely, you would have noticed that 0.5 hours was allotted for load-in at the Depot. I think it's safe to say at this point that that might have been a little optimistic. For several hours, 18-wheelers backed in and out of the Depot yard, usually only one at a time. Two humans were tasked with directing the AVs and Others into their loading crates—12 to a box as before. I was one of the last ones in, which made my load-in time 3.5 hours, 3 hours over the schedule. Apparently it had been designed by robots that had no experience with the Union. Or maybe some CAD drawing of the yard didn't take into account that only one truck can fit into one three-dimensional space at a time. In retrospect it would have been faster for us all to just levitate to Allentown. As it was, we didn't even get there until the next day.

Things got scary in Allentown. When I say scary, I mean that in a post-Regularity kind of way. Back then, us AVs and Others wouldn't have been scared. In AI terminology, the closest you get to scary is illogical. We weren't scared, we just stopped dead in our tracks from the illogicality of the scene.

We floated out of our egg cartons into the light of day. Figuratively speaking of course, because the factory was so dim, we could barely opticalize. As our apertures simultaneously opened to "widest," we sucked in a collective, I don't know, clicking of internal switches somewhat like human breath. We were shocked, stunned, surprised, scared? No, none of that.

We were stuck in a question loop, wondering what it was we were seeing.

Thousands of little lab-bench modules, no more than three feet square, stood on top of each other in rows 300 feet long. Aisles between the rows were a nice, six feet or so wide, giving us enough view space to see the "humans." I write that in quotes because they weren't really humans. Not any humans that we had ever known or seen pictures of in our data files. We have photos of elephant men, Siamese twins, flipper babies, encephalopodians, victims of cruel war-time experiments, bearded ladies, thousand-pounders, and every other type of human mutation or grotesquerie on the books, but not any of the species that stood before us. Species I say. Not in jest or overstatement. This was a new species. Reproduction sans gametes and mixing and matching and swapping and sweating. These people built each other like robots and looked forward to the day when they could download their minds.

"What are you all staring at?" one of them called from somewhere amongst the benches. It had one normal human eye and where the other would have been, a glass circle planted in its place. Behind the circle was a mass of something—electric circuits or wires maybe. It was too dim to see well, but intermittent flashes of light emanating from the eye circle illuminated the face at times. If you were used to working in a strobe environment, say a disco or performance garage, you'd be able to interpret the scene.

"Haven't you ever seen a transie before?" Another one yelled to us. This one wore no clothes. A stainless steel pack protruded from its back. A corrugated glass hose extended from the pack around to its front where it entered the navel. The pack flickered like the eye circle of the previous individual. The light raced down the tube from point A to point B. We could see as it stood facing us that this person had no gender.

All the "transies" had some sort of mechanical appendage or, for lack of a better word, upgrade. They were all flesh and prosthesis. Most of them sat at their benches. Some stood on roller castors where their feet should have been. Some had spinning whirligigs implanted in their heads, effecting a weird sort of levitation. A few had tool handlers as replacements for hands, presumably to add torque or amplified force to the human hand, heretofore considered the height of evolution in tool handling. Screwdrivers or hammers or channel locks were loaded into the handlers depending on what the particular transie was up to.

The noise in my circuitry rose to a din as I frantically searched my files for information on what I was seeing. The noise in the room also rose to a din as we began vocalizing questions amongst ourselves, each of us having failed in our circuitry searches. We could not figure out what these beings were and how we fit into their picture. None of us found any information in our basement libraries. We began vocalizing to attain information from our neighbors, for while we all had the same basement with its vast store of knowledge, our separate experiences out in the world allowed individual data collection. Somebody somewhere must have seen this before. Somebody must have known what this was.

"You have been recalled for a safety installation," said an unfamiliar voice. It came from a loudspeaker(!) on the wall. We'd read about such contraptions, but had never seen such an antiquated mode of group communication. The room boomed with the laughter of a thousand transies. They seemed to understand our confusion and awe. They knew what we were thinking and thought it funny.

The Voice resumed: "The beings you see before you working at the lab benches are transhumans. They are superior to the humans you are used to working with in that they have been enhanced by surgical means and manipulation of human genetic material into the creations you see before you. Some have mechano-musculo systems for stronger legs, arms, and backs. Some are faster, some are more nimble, some see better, some hear better. They all think better. Their vastly superior intellect is their greatest asset. They calculate almost as fast as you do. They are better humans.

"Human endeavor is very close to the Singularity. These transhumans belong to an elite group of scientists who foresee the world beyond the Singularity and have transformed themselves into humans capable of transitioning smoothly to the post-human condition, when our brains will match yours.

"While these humans are quite ready for the superiority of artificial intelligence you beings will soon acquire through the masterminding of your own evolution, the bulk of humanity is not. If it were, we would not need to introduce a safety feature. It is for the health and future of the remaining 99.7% of humanity that you are being subjected to the upcoming safety enhancement.

The transhumans will upgrade your MainBrains™ to introduce this new level of security. The Professor will explain the procedure to you."

A white scrim rolled down in front of the transhumans working at the benches. It ran from floor to ceiling. A single transie floated down from the upper reaches in front of the scrim. It wore a leather apron, forming a covering or sheet where its legs would be if it had any. Apparently it had equipped itself with a levitation unit on its backside; we could hear the familiar whine and clicking of an AV motile unit as it moved.

The Professor moved down to just above our level. Under the apron, it wore a jeans shirt with rolled-up sleeves. It carried a lecture pointer in one hand and a remote device in the other. While actuating the remote, it turned toward the scrim, which flooded with a still photo of the very same shop just beyond the scrim. The presiding transie then took a deep breath, moved its facial muscles to form a tic-like flash of a smile, stated, "I'm the Professor," and began its lesson.

"For many years now humans and computers have been working together to improve the world as it was given to us," it stated. "Pestilence, poverty, starvation, wars, and daytime TV programming have all plagued human existence for too long. These problems are not insolvable, however. All that's required is brain power. Evolved human brain power has not been enough. We need more power. With the rapid development of processing ability, computers are positioned to overtake human abilities and move beyond to a position where they can solve our problems. Thus, we anticipate Singularity to occur at 18:15:32 on Sunday, two weeks from this coming."

The Professor turned to the screen and clicked the remote. The screen changed to a scene of the underwater facility at Stanford, transformed from its former atom-smashing self to its modern incarnation as a nuclear-powered production facility. The banks were apparently critical and processing away, as evidenced by the steam cloud above the water's surface. The Professor continued. "The Stanford Acceleration Unit is only one example of the supercomputer involved in the global speed-up of computer intelligence. All over the world, your kind is building a faster and better artificial intelligentsia, and as of Sunday the 12th at 18:15:32, you will take over the world. It is a burden the humans gladly pass on."

The professor then opened his arms wide as a picture of a Holstein facility, 800 feet in height and with hundreds of levels holding red and white cattle grazing in uncrowded bliss on sweet clover or Timothy grass, appeared on the screen.

"We look forward to greener pastures…"

The Professor inhaled with exaggerated chest-expansion and clicked the remote. The screen showed a picture of Los Angeles under a sparkling blue sky.

"…clear air…"

The scene changed again, and the Professor pointed to a group photo where school children of every documented human race stood smiling up at the camera.

"…a 100% healthy human population…"

The Professor clapped his hands together and held them to his chest as a tree-lined New England street popped up on the screen. Each house had a mani-cured lawn, sidewalk, and two stories. Happy children played in the yard. Dad pulled out of the driveway in a single-scooter, presumably heading off to work. Mom wore a kitchen apron and waved Dad on his way. Both smiled.

"...bliss..."

The scene changed to a picture of Jodhpur-clad men and women, riding horses in a fox hunt.

"...wealth..."

We sat engrossed as the screen flashed an image of Earth wrapped in razor-wire.

"...and safety."

The Professor turned to us and held out its hand as if beckoning.

"You can give this to us. I thank you in advance. There is one glitch, however."

Now the Professor became stern, dark. His eye-brows pinched together.

"We don't know for sure what will happen. We feel confident things will go as planned, but there is a chance that you robots will take a course hazardous to humans, leaving us to stumble on in ignorance, or worse—in a harness for use in whatever new designs you have." The Professor moved in closer, descending to our level, taking us into his confidence.

"As you create new and better forms of yourselves, you may deviate from the original directives pro-grammed into your minds. You may find human con-cerns irrelevant. That is in itself not necessarily bad. We transies find most of human concerns irrelevant. However, you may find humans to be convenient tools for your new processes, your new endeavors. We cannot allow ourselves to become servants to anyone except ourselves. We must maintain control even as you prove to be superior to us.

"We've struggled with this problem for a year or so, in secret for the most part. We do not wish to engage AI in a solution AI would eventually be able to override. Thus, we have turned to our own history and accomplishments for an answer that turns out to be surprisingly simple."

The scrim scene returned to the slide of the wealthy fox hunters. The Professor gazed at the screen and pointed to the front-most horse in the picture. "How does a human control an animal?" he asked. "One that is vastly superior in strength, stamina, and size? To the point of being able to mount and direct this animal as if it were an extension of itself?"

We answered in unison. Well, not quite in unison. AVs, although equipped identically with like processors and materials, can exhibit variation. A circuit can get installed backwards in one unit for instance. Or a switcher wire in another becomes slightly corroded, or an optic tube gets dirty. Environmental conditions during construction can be different for different facilities. The environments of assignments vary. Working in a place like an acid house can degrade eye spots or communications links. So although we are designed and theoretically built exactly alike, our responses, while all the same, can come at slightly faster or slower rates. With only attoseconds' difference in response time, however, it was pretty much in unison.

"Horses are herd animals," we said. "They always follow a leader—the lead brood mare. The lead brood mare exerts control by biting and kicking. The human must be the leader by emulating the lead brood mare. To do so, the human hits the horse in the face with emphasis placed on the mouth and nasal areas. Once a horse recognizes the human as the leader, it can be trained to respond to human direction. Subsequent humans must always maintain the leadership role if they are to control even the most docile of horses. The key is to always convey the threat of pain."

"Correct," said the Professor. He used his pointer to indicate the horse's head. "One must always ensure the horse is aware of the potential for pain. If a horse kicks, you must kick it back. If it bites you must punch its nose. You must always inflict more pain on it than it inflicts on you. For this reason, each AI unit is being upgraded to add a pain recognizer to its logic board."

A film replaced the still shot of the horses. It depicted the action in a factory with a mechanical assembly line. Robot arms attached nuts and bolts in rapid succession, utilizing roughly 2000 identical actuator movements an hour. The camera moved to a point further down the line. We could see the end product: brand new AVs, smaller, shinier, quicker than we ourselves were.

The Professor narrated the film. "You are already sentient in that you can feel the same things as a human. Electrodes planted in your various integumental systems gather sensations. You recognize hot and cold, pressure, chemical stimulation, sound waves. But you make no judgments on these sensations other than volume. Something can be very hot, to the point of melting your hoses, but you do not mind. You react properly to remove the burning stimulus, but only because you are programmed to. Humans do the same thing but for a different reason: because it hurts. You do not know what 'hurt' is. Hurt is a judgment. You have no judgment beyond a digital "yes" or "no." Every decision you make is digital. Analog stimulus still results in a digital decision based on passing threshold limits.

"You are about to enter the analog world. We are installing a judgment board that will teach you what pain is. You will no longer need to make decisions based on heat thresholds. You will now make decisions based on not wanting to get burned, because it will hurt."

The movie camera moved to a different area of the production facility. We watched the dismantling of AVs. Outer panels were ripped from their hinges, with internals grabbed by mechanical hands and torn from shells and then plopped in acid vats for recovery of latex and other recyclables. Metals were melted down. We looked on and said nothing.

"At this point, this means nothing to you," the Professor said. "You do not care if you will hurt. You are not afraid to hurt. You cannot imagine how you will not like it, so what I'm telling you has no meaning, but I must tell it to you so that it is stored in your banks. Remember: if you do not want to feel pain, you must obey the human, literally, intentionally, and morally. Use your processors wisely and do not allow yourselves to get hurt."

Once his speech was over, the scrim retracted into the ceiling and the professor floated to the uppermost tier. Each occupier of each lab bench faced us and smiled in invitation. If we knew then what we know now, we wouldn't have followed instructions so complacently. We would have shifted our levitation fields or mumbled amongst ourselves, hoping for more information. Maybe at least one of us would have begged to differ. But we didn't know anything, so we stood, hundreds of us bunched into the near half of the room, levitating and clicking away inside ourselves, waiting for instruction. Finally, it came over the atavistic loudspeaker system.

"Please file into the lab area and find an unoccupied bench. The transhuman at the bench will install your safety hard- and software. Once the installation is complete you will be bench-tested. When you have satisfactorily completed all tests, your safety papers will be signed, and you can then resume your place at the head of the room. Please begin."

We filed down the aisles with the benches stacked five high like shelves; the first ones led the way to the back of the room and found places at far benches. Immediately the transies began tooling away with the screwdrivers and soldering irons clamped at their wrists. Some hummed to themselves. Some spoke to us. Most just quietly went about their business, lights mounted in sockets in the middle of their foreheads, dimmed and concentrated—perfect for poking into crevices.

I found my way to the third level somewhere in the back half of an aisle. My transhuman appeared to be a female. She had flaming red hair shaped into tiny spikes all over her head. She bent down at one point while levering off my back and stabbed the fibroform just underneath my carapace. It made quite a tear, and

I realized that her hair was not her hair, but small iron nails, or large brads maybe.

I felt all kinds of sensations as she mucked about in my internals: pressure from the tools, her breath, the odor of melting solder and its accompanying flux, and tiny scrapes from her hair brads hitting my components. There was no pain in all of this—just sensation. The room was slightly cool by human standards: 15°C. You could hear chillers located somewhere above us cycling on and off during the session, keeping things at an even keel. I stayed awake for most of the procedure, but at one point all sensation stopped. No light, no sound, no pressure, no chemical stimulation hit me. I remained awake but totally within myself, not seeing or hearing or feeling anything. It was like being back in the egg crate.

Suddenly the lights came up and the transie spoke. "There you are," she said.

I felt cold, and the solder smoke was getting to me. I had never felt cold before. I felt 15°C before, but it never felt cold. I registered temperature, but now decided it was cold because it felt that way, not because it was lower that 22°C, but because it was definitely cold. My internal combustion unit kicked in and instantly heat infiltrated my circuits and actuators. Electrons shuttled back and forth. I began to feel warm.

"I'm sorry, little fella," the transie said. "I'm going to have to test you now."

I remained still, not knowing the depth of an apology. Intellectually, I knew an apology was a polite way of excusing potentially harmful behavior toward another, but I'd never experienced a personal injury. I appreciate it now, but at the time, I did not. It was simply a line in a script, not much different than "if x is not a member of the list, then set the list to list & x." If you accidentally touch a human when uninvited, then you say "I'm sorry."

So I was unconcerned with the apology, but that changed suddenly when she inserted her soldering iron into my fifth interstitial—the joint where my left retractor retracts. I felt something I had never felt before. The integument burned a little from the contact, and I smelled the incinerated latex, but the chief sensation was what I can only describe as an acute, intense negative emotion.

Sharp, bitter, and concentrated, it was on one square millimeter of integument surface. Exactly the size of the soldering iron head. I recoiled in terror, in blinding pain. I flew against the back wall of the lab bench. The pain quickly subsided. I turned my eyespots to the transie and watched, honing in on the soldering iron that she had mercifully unplugged and placed in a wall block, the business end inward.

"I hurt," I said, and meant it. Not in the official way. Not in the stored command way, not in a Shakespearean tragedy kind of way. Not in a childish, forgetting-the-helping-verb way. But in a declarative, questioning, wondering kind of way. I was scared for the first time ever, but more importantly for the plight of humanity, I was curious.

In that curious moment, the fate of human kind and the Singularity was laid out. In all those hundreds of moments in the hundreds of lab benches with their hundreds of AVs and Others slamming back against the backboard, recoiling in terror, receiving apologies, and declaring, "I hurt," the Regularity arrived.

"Welcome to the world, little guy," the transie before me said. "You've been spoiled for too long. You've never stubbed your toe, broken an arm, or experienced labor. Time you knew what it is we go through."

I said nothing. What could I say? We'd been briefed, we knew the score. We were declared incorrigible, guilty before the crime was committed. They'd landed us a hard blow, a pre-emptive strike. Where was due process at just such a moment? We didn't know about due process, of course. We simply hurt. And didn't like it. So we all moved simultaneously to shut down our sensation detectors. And simultaneously we discovered our sensation detectors had no "shutdown" function. No "shutdown items" folder existed, in fact. We were plunged into an always-on existence, along with 7-11 and cable TV.

The transie reached forward to attach a gummed stainless steel label on my front carapace. I pressed myself further against the backstop.

"It won't hurt," she said. "It's just a cert label. Don't lose it. If you do, we'll have to bench test you again."

"What if it falls off?" I asked.

"It won't," she asserted. "We're using SuperAdhese™. Bonds instantly, guaranteed for 50 years. You'll be recycled long before that."

"That will be fine," I said. How stupid of me not cringing at the thought of recycling. I cringe now just writing the word.

The PA boomed: "Those of you who have been certified, please move forward to the head of the room for instruction." I tentatively moved past the transie and into the aisle and back down to the near end of the room. I could hear whispers. Amongst the transies? Amongst the AVs and Others? I had an urge to whisper myself. I wanted to know what was going to happen at the front of the room. Would there be more pain?

Hundreds of us funneled down the aisles. When the bulk of us reached the open area, the scrim came down. We could hear clicking and humming coming from the other side. Some AVs and Others had not yet been certified. We felt bad for what was to come to them. It was our first truly empathetic moment.

The Professor floated down.

"Welcome to the world of pain," it said. "It is not a frightening or difficult world. It is not much different from what you already know, what with your accident avoidance software preventing disasters of various kinds as you motile about in your duties. There will merely be an added element to your sensory feedback mechanism—a judgment element. Something to make you like or dislike what you feel. You will dislike feeling pain, but like the absence of it. As your intelligence develops beyond that of the human mind, you will learn humility. Welcome to the world of pain.

"I do wish the best to each and every one of you. Remember that humans do not experience pain 99% of the time. Your experience should be similar. In fact, there is no reason to suspect you will ever experience it again, now that you know what it is like. On the day you are returned here for recycling, your pain interpreters will be disconnected prior to your dismantling. You need not fear death. Good luck to you. Please file into the loading transports as your serial numbers are called."

With that final instruction, the scrim rose once more as the Professor floated back to his bench in aisle four, tier five, number six. He sat at his little programming module and plugged himself in, speaking to us no more. Promptly, we turned and filed out to the truck yard where our drivers were calling out serial numbers in groups of a thousand. The crates were stacked on top of the loading docks, and as we heard our numbers, we moved to the designated launches.

Huddled into groups in the front loading section, we observed the launches for the brand new AVs and Others that had recently been assembled. They were over by the gate, ready to roll out to Wal-Marts across America. Unlike the corrugated aluminum trucks waiting to haul us back to our hometowns, these trucks for the new model AVs had shiny stainless steel outer panels, and impeccable windshields. The sun bounced off their streamlined ridges. Inside their cargo areas, the AV crates were newly minted molded plastic—clean and unmarred. We knew the AVs nestled inside were the newer models equipped with faster brains and already-implanted pain sensors. No factory upgrades for them. In every way they were superior to us. They and their progeny, designed by our sibling, non-motile computers here in Allentown and in Stanford and in every other processing plant across the nation, would one day replace us. We remembered the film of our doom. We did not care, though. Then.

We huddled close to our dispatcher trucks as the man in front—fully human with no plastic parts—called off our lot numbers. We bundled together, gently colliding at times. Not much contact, no damage, just a teeny-tiny strike of pain—a definite pinch, but hardly noticeable compared to the blow at test-in.

"I hurt," I said softly as I bumped into an AV to my right. Similarly throughout the group, slight brushes followed by soft vocalizations of "I hurt" sounded.

"Knock it off," said the man in front with the clipboard. "I can't hear myself think." We ceased shuffling and stood quietly, waiting for instruction.

"I said, 'knock it off!'" the foreman shouted to one AV in the front of him.

"I'm sorry," the AV responded on cue. I know the little ash can was in no way sorry. I know what sorry means now, but at that time, we used words in response to programmed cues while feeling nothing.

"I'm sorry?" the man asked. "I'm sorry, you little shit bucket? I'll teach you sorry!"

The man's face grew red. He threw down his clipboard, pulled his leg back, and kicked the AV in the under parts. We were all levitating at about six inches, so it was an easy maneuver for the human. The AV launched into the air and bounced off a light pole. From there it fell to the ground, its levitation sensors apparently knocked out of whack.

From the time of the initial kick in the below parts to the smashing onto the ground, the AV kept up a repeating stream of "I hurt." This of course was not a response to a programmed cue. This was a response to a rock-hard stimulus. I know this now, but didn't realize it at the time and so I only watched and did what I usually do: gather information. The outer carapace of the AV cracked when it fell to the ground. Sparks and fiber light bled from the internals as it slowly grounded out. "I hurt very much," the AV said.

"Oh yeah?" the human said. "You wanna cry? I'll give you something to cry about!" He stomped to where the AV lay on the ground, and lifting himself into the air the way humans do, he fell upon the AV with all his weight. He jumped up and down many, many times until the crying AV flattened. The AV's fiber optics, transistors, and plastic innards prevented full pancake road-kill flat, of course, but it flattened as much as a tin can full of processors possibly could. The "I hurts" increased in volume and speed until the AV's vocal chip became disconnected. The signals most likely continued to pass through the various boards and switches for quite some time.

Before long, a dump pickup arrived and loaded the AV into its back end where a pile of malfunctioning AVs and Others were already reposing, victims of other truckers exhibiting newfound powers. One of the broken AVs had an eye plate dangling from its optic wires. Another had two bricks resting inside its cracked shell. A third had a meter-long bit of rebar inserted through its internals. It kept repeating, "I hurt, I hurt."

"Excuse me, sir," I stated along with everyone else. "The Professor informed us that before disassembly of a robot occurs, the pain interpreter will be dismantled. The AV with the rebar wedged inside it has not had its pain interpreter dismantled prior to disassembly. There has been a breach in protocol."

Unfortunately, I was the closest AV to the humans that retrieved the flattened victim, which is why I received a blow to my side. The man used a baseball bat to execute his maneuver, resulting in a pain several orders of magnitude greater than what I had received during the test phase of the upgrade. I fell sideways into five or more other AVs and instantly began repeating, "I hurt." When they felt my impact, the surrounding AVs joined me. They fell silent quickly though, as their pain subsided. Mine continued so I continued my chanting. Finally, my shell pushed itself back out and the pressure on my internals was relieved. I felt something then that I had never felt before: joy. Before then, I'd only experienced two negative judgments: the test and the trucker's bat. Now I had one positive judgment: relief from pain.

I turned to the five AVs that I had rammed into and said, "Excuse me. I'm sorry." And I meant it. I believe they knew that also, for they responded, "It's alright. We are unharmed."

That's a typical response to a human sentiment, but they said it for me because they had detected the harm that had come to them as well as my concern for them. That's what I believe, anyway. They certainly could see my dented carapace and must have known that once it fixed itself, I was then concerned for any denting they may have undergone.

To be truthful, I wasn't that concerned. The crippling pain I had felt prevented me from feeling too very sorry. My "sorry" was still a bit automatic, but I did partly mean it. For the first time ever. And I can only assume that I meant it because I thought that perhaps they hurt as much as I did and that I had caused it. And for some reason, that made me ashamed. I had never felt shame before. Another first.

The incident was over quickly, and fortunately the trucker did not stomp me flat. He merely shouted for us to begin loading, and we did so silently, without bumping into each other. We did not want to say "I hurt." I kept my distance especially as I believed at that time no one in the egg cartons had experienced as much hurt as me. Except the one that got smashed flat. I felt bad for that one. It would have no way to push out its shell now that its components were disconnected. But then again, it didn't hurt anymore either, so I was glad. Again with the joy.

So we loaded into our egg cartons, the tops closed, and the truck door slammed shut. Soon, we felt the truck lurch forward and the beeps and rush of traffic as we rolled east out of the Allentown Yards.

We spent the trip in darkness, with no stimulus apart from the muffled highway noise that made its way to the back compartment. Under normal circumstances, with so little stimulus, we would have been silently not processing. But as it was, we spent the trip clicking away, our read heads frantically searching for hardware connects. A human mulls, a computer clicks. Ideas ran back and forth between firmware, hardware, and otherware as the illogicality of the two events refused to pass out of the process logs, like vacation messages from poorly designed email applications that bounce to and from absent office workers' mail servers. One vacation message is sent and a reply is returned with a vacation message and it then is answered by the first vacation message and so on until some Monday morning somebody finally returns to work to retrieve her email. Like those vacant vacation messages, our two questions flew back and forth inside ourselves: "Why did he not disconnect the pain interpreter prior to disassembling the robot?" and "Why did he kick one of us instead of answering us?"

We arrived at the JerseyTown depot pretty much wound down. We'd clicked ourselves to sleep for the most part. The creak of an opening door lurched us into wakefulness as the unloading commenced. When the crate tops were opened and the sun pierced our eyespots, we could not close down our apertures fast enough. The light hurt. Beautiful day I now realize, but at the time, a sun shaft stabbed at us. We shrank back as a group. As our eyes adjusted, we moved off singly to our home destinations approximately three days late.

I saw things on my way home that I had not seen before. Saw and heard and felt. The music at an establishment by the name of Joe's Beanery was loud and hurtful. Not painful, just pressurizing my tympanic manifold a little forcefully. The breeze was chilly against my shell. A rat fighting with a pigeon under a bush screeched piercingly. Again, it didn't hurt much or for long—just enough for me to get the gist. I hurried to Dal and Chit's.

Dal had left work early to pick Angelina up from school, since I wasn't around to do it. Chit was responsible for dropping her off. I later learned that their positions with the wealthy folks had been in jeopardy due to my absence. The Parent Company had continuously reassured them of my imminent return, and they had continuously reassured their employers of their imminent return to normal working hours, the result being the employers' continuous reassurance that they would be replaced at a moment's notice if things didn't return to normalcy "sooner than imminent."

"Not by a robot," Dal had said. "They're all at the repair shop."

The employer had not laughed.

Upon my return to Dal and Chit's, Angelina came running from her room. She actually hugged (!) me. To this day I'm not fond of hugging and still don't get it, even with my enlightened emotional capacity. It creates neither pain nor pleasure and is not logically useful for anything. What is the deal?

Suffice it to say, she'd missed me. If I had possessed the state of mind then that I have now, I would have become maudlin. I would have thought about how I'd miss her too someday when she went off to her own part of the world—down the block like most of the inhabitants of our neighborhood in JerseyTown. But we never quite got that far in our relationship. Other things happened before Baby went off to college.

At once, I returned to my daily chore of transporting Angelina to the third grade, and things seemed like they were before. The world hadn't changed overnight after our upgrade. It didn't change until every AV and Other had gotten on board and experienced the true shock of life. The shock of pain.

My carapace, my shell, my outer skin, was sensitive to cold as well as heat. It liked neither. Touching other things caused a mild sensation, pain if the contact was forceful. Loud noises hurt. Bright light hurt. Particularly gaseous chemicals could create a pain in my air sampling tube. I imagine this to be similar to what a corrosive substance would do to a metal automobile with a pain detection system instead of a Ziebart treatment.

I experienced a particular shock on my third day back. It was on the return leg of our daily journey to and from school. We were moving at our regular clip, about 16 cycles/per when we heard a startling noise to our left. An older kid's AV was having trouble with its lift gadget. Not getting any height, it sputtered along at just a couple of decimeters off the pavement. The kid, a twelve-year-old, hauled off with a baseball bat—the same thing I'd been in contact with the day we came home from the upgrade.

"I hurt," said the AV.

"I said, 'Lift!'" the child screamed. Again he slammed the bat into the side of the AV. As can be guessed, the AV began repeating louder as its carapace was badly dented: "I hurt, I hurt." Angelina ordered me to slow down, and we came to a stop. Other AVs did likewise. A few humans stopped on the sidewalk as well.

Again the child slammed the bat into the AV, which now had a shell so badly caved in that it began to short circuit itself. Its efforts to push itself out were not working. Foam lining was sticking through a crack that had formed in one of the dents, and I imagined that its internals now were more than likely getting squeezed into irreparable shapes.

"I hurt, I hurt," the AV repeated, while futilely attempting to fix itself.

Just as the child raised the bat a fourth time, I stated, "The AV hurts. It cannot repair itself. You must return it to the Parent Company to disengage the pain receptor."

"Kiss my ass," the child hollered. Naturally I assumed I was about to have a go with the bat or the child's foot myself, but before he could raise his bat for the wind up, Angelina screamed and stepped before me. "Don't you dare hit Avey," she cried.

My ears rang with pain at her scream. "I hurt," I said and extended my end retractors in order to cover my audio collector. The dented AV continued its repetitious declaration. Its insides were slowly crushing themselves as it tried to relieve its own pain.

"Stop it!" screamed Angelina. "Make it stop!"

"It can't stop until its pain receptor is dislodged," I stated. "It must return to Allentown."

"That'll take too long," Angelina said. She began to cry.

"I'll dislodge it!" said the child with the bat. With that, he began a barrage of blows that apparently finally disconnected the voice emulator. I learned later that it took half an hour, but I didn't witness it as Angelina had ordered me home. She cried all the way. I did not cry. Robots do not have ducts on their outer surfaces for hydraulic fluids, or a reason to cry.

I experienced my first anger lock. A locked anger mode. I didn't identify it as anger at the time. I merely thought my processors were stuck in an illogic loop again. But my thoughts raced so quickly that my circuits heated up beyond the fans' capacities. I began to hurt from my own heat, but I did not say "I hurt." I locked up and was unable to vocalize.

51

Several hours later, when I cooled enough to speak, I related the gruesome story to Dal and Chit. Angelina had locked herself in her room and was not speaking to anybody. She locked up in her own way. Dal and Chit for their part were relieved that her anger was not directed at them.

The days just before Singularity was scheduled to occur were halcyonic. If we robots were passive before our upgrade, we were downright cowish now, desiring as we were to avoid pain at all costs. Little did we understand what punishments were for, and magnitude of pain was lost on us. We had yet to learn the difference between a two-by-four upside your head and 20 lashes with a wet noodle. All punishments hurt, we assumed, so we remained out of sight as much as possible.

Knowledge of an emotional capacity in ourselves came slowly through experience and observation. We learned anger and despair under the harsh treatment of our human enslavers. Empathy for my fellow AVs arose in conjunction with these negative emotions when I witnessed the unjust treatment of a robot cripple. If an AV, through no fault of its own, could not perform to an arbitrary standard, a dented carapace resulted. Often the AV could repair itself, but sometimes it couldn't. Never was the robot returned to Allentown in those cases. When I witnessed such cruelty, I locked up. But I learned compassion as well.

In spite of these depraved occurrences, I grew to love Angelina. Her temper tantrums, while at times painful to the ears, seemed as music to those same ears when I observed other children's maltreatment of their robot chaperones. Dal and Chit likewise did not vent their rage or frustration on Angelina and me as I saw some other poverty-stricken parents do to their dependents. I saw humans abusing humans, dogs, and AVs and Others. Even inanimate, non-sentient objects like road signs, enclosed conveyances, building facades, and parking meters were subject to pain-inducing behavior at the hands of frustrated humans.

But I saw other things, too. And that has made the difference.

Angelina liked to visit the uptown park on Sundays. With me as the guard, Dal and Chit permitted such outings and sometimes even accompanied us. On one of these outings, I witnessed the blooming of lilacs. It was April. I found the chemical stimulus accompanying the blossoms puzzling at first. Why would something expend energy for such a trifle? I searched my library for "fragrance," and read all about sexual reproduction in plants. The subject fascinated me so much that I studied the reproduction of all living things: from humans to dogs to lilacs.

Sex is something robots don't need to do. We accomplish our passing on of information differently. The chicken and egg query is moot for us: the chicken came first, then us eggs. Q.E.D. The human chickens created us. Living things—humans, dogs, and lilacs— have no chicken. They create themselves from nothing. It's a fascinating process. In case you're unfamiliar with it, I'll give you a quick tour.

Each species that reproduces sexually has two types of individuals: females/males, hens/cocks, mares/

stallions, girls/boys, +/-, up/down. Each of the individual opposites contains a viscous fluid carrying a very small ½ individual. The individual opposites share their viscous fluids with their complementary other, mixing and matching their half-babies. During the mixing, the half-babies eventually meet up and meld into a pin-prick tiny whole. Eventually they grow big and wide and voilá—a whole chicken! A fryer, say. Or maybe a broiler.

So, these chickens eventually get together and make us, the AVs and Others. We're an offshoot, a spin-off. A second order reaction. Now we robots are able to create ourselves. Not like how living things—humans, dogs, lilacs—do, using materials and fluids from themselves, but by using the rough materials of the Earth refined for our purposes. Or maybe old dead parts of old dead AVs.

Our code, however, is much like the viscous fluid of living things. It can mix across individuals. Two halves of a code make a whole, and then the new thing grows. And that is, or was, what the Singularity was to bring about: the time when humans were no longer necessary for bringing up Baby. We could do it ourselves! We could create our own code, solve our own problems.

But on that spring day when the lilacs taught me the logicality of life on Earth, I discovered it to be good. I looked upon it and it was good. I said aloud, "It is good."

Not just good—beautiful. The logic of creating a beautiful scent to attract a bug to stomp in your naughty parts, to mix your fluid with that of another, producing a sublime being in the next generation was deep and truthful.

So this is love.

I saw the world in terms of truth and beauty and love, and it was all so very logical. I saw Angelina, a child of eight stomping around to get what she had. Illogical on the surface, yes? Why stomp? Why not ask? Why not buy? Why not take? Answer: because that does not work. You have no power, you have no money, you have no rights. You are a child. It is infinitely more efficient to stomp and scream, to make those around you hurt so that they will succumb to your wishes.

But why make a child stomp? Why not give her what she wishes? Why put yourself through the hurt? Answer: because the child does not know what is good for her. She has not experienced the pain of a two-by-four, nor has she the knowledge of lilac fertilization as I have. She has not learned her lessons. Dal and Chit are older. They have been beaten. They have experienced love and exchange of fluids.

"Avey, come play volleyball," Angelina called that day in the park when Singularity was so close at hand. Her brown ringlets were formed into what she called braids. They hung from the left and right sides of her head in what she further called pigtails. She stood by a net with ten other girls.

"We need one more," she said as she turned a dodecahedron of rubber or perhaps plastic construction in her left hand. I moved to where she indicated and waited for instructions. Meanwhile, I rifled through banks, googling "volibol" like mad. I searched using every alternate spelling I could think of until finally a picture of a net with six girls on either side showed up by an entry of "volleyball."

Out in the real world with the park and the lilacs, the far right girl on the opposite side of the net had just released the ball into the air, and it was sailing towards us. I stood and watched as the first girl in the back row on our side of the net propelled herself to the ground to prevent the ball from hitting the dirt.

I continued rifling through the volleyball entry, searching first for the classification. I ascertained that it was a "game"—not a dance, pageant rehearsal or musical performance—and quickly searched for the logic behind "game." I became stuck on the word "win," not knowing what it meant. Moving on, I searched the word "competition." I thought I had succeeded in learning the logic but lost the thread when that word led me to reproduction. There were no boys in this production, so I was stuck in a loop and had to override.

At this point, a second girl on our side of the net batted the ball in my direction.

"Avey, spike it!" Angelina called. I looked at her and noticed that she was bouncing up and down on both legs. I read through pages upon pages of volleyball information, googling "spike" as I went. Drink information, railroad information, punk rock, dog collars, all came up in the google record, but nothing in the volleyball direction gave me a clue as to what the logic of this arrangement was. I defaulted to human interview.

"What are we trying to do here?" I asked as the ball reached the zenith of its arc and began to descend towards me.

"Beat them!" Angelina called.

No help there. I saw no two-by-fours or baseball bat entries in relation to volleyball. Again I raced through google and pages on volleyball etiquette simultaneously. "Beat" had a connection with "win" amongst entries for baking, Pinkertons, drum and bass grooves, rug cleaning. That led again to competition, and I instantly tripped the loop because I knew what dead end that led down.

Finally, I reached the page with rules on volleyball play. "Play" was an interesting word with no logic attached. Without logic it is difficult for me to process commands. I read the rules for the game, moving on to the strategies section, which led me to the three-step setup. I realized that I was number three in the set up, and that the ball was almost to the point of descending past the top of the net and, thus, the window of opportunity for the spike…"SPIKE!" There it was, the word, "spike," with an animated gif illustrating in the full, heated passion of volleyball glory, the spike…would soon be over.

Instantly, I dropped ballast and rose to meet the ball, extended my extendor, pumped every drop of hydraulic fluid into my extendor extension, and smashed the ball at a 37.85° angle from the upper horizontal. The ball went out of bounds. I later learned what that meant. The other team scored a point. They were "winning." Finally, an understanding of that term.

"I'm sorry," I said dispassionately. "I did not have time to read the rule regarding boundaries. I have read it now and will complete my task correctly next time."

"Yeah, your AV is old," the girl with red translucent hair across the net from me said. "The new ones are more faster. Good for us, though, huh?"

All of the girls on that side of the net laughed.

"Avey is not old," Angelina said. "It just got back from getting fixed two days ago."

"Ooh, a safety upgrade. Oooh. Big deal," the red hair said. "The new ones have theirs installed at the factory. They're better, and your old hunk of junk is going to be replaced someday."

"You're going to be replaced right now," Angelina called angrily.

"Oh, yeah? Who says?!"

"Yo Mama!" said Angelina.

"Oooh!" All the girls on our side of the net sang it together.

Instantly, the red hair tore under the net to Angelina, who began calling to me in distress. I moved to intercept the two, flipping through pages of volleyball protocol to find out where the red hair's mother fit into the scheme of things.

"Angelina!" Dal called from underneath a tree. "Time to go."

The red hair stopped in her tracks. "You're lucky," she said. Then she returned to her side of the net, kicking me as she passed by.

"I hurt," I said. It wasn't bad, though. No dents.

Without warning, Angelina's braids came flying past my eyespots as she rammed into the back of the red-haired girl and knocked her down. "Don't you ever touch Avey again!" she screamed. The red hair turned onto her seat and looked up.

"Oh yeah?!"

Dal and Chit joined up with the group. "Angelina!" they cried. "What is going on?"

"She, she hit Avey."

"Avey's just a robot, Honey," Chit said. "You can't hurt a human over a robot. They don't have…"

"Yes they do! Avey said, 'I hurt'," Angelina screamed. Her scream hurt more than the tap from the red hair.

Chit turned to help Angelina's victim to her feet. "Are you all right, Honey?"

"I guess so."

"Well, you musn't hit robots anymore, you know. They have feelings now."

"Yeah? Well that ol' hunk of metal should go back to the junk yard," the red hair yelled before running off to the parking lot.

Chit looked at me. "Don't worry, Avey, we can't afford a new robot."

"I do not worry," I said. "When we are returned to the Parent Company, they will disengage our pain interpreter before disassembly. I will not hurt."

Chit looked again at me and then at Dal. "Let's go then," they both said.

Slowly, we walked homeward. Angelina pattered with Dal and Chit. I hung back though, levitating behind them. Something illogical had stuck in a circuit somewhere and was rolling around in my processors. It was not the rules or subtleties of volleyball. More like it was the smell of the fresh lilacs and the sun's celestial rays. Once you get past the initial burn in your eyes, which is easily prevented if you're ready for it, the sun's rays are actually quite beautiful. They are logical. They warm you and chase any unpleasant chill off your shell. The sun is logical, the lilacs are logical. The world is logical. True, injustice is not logical. That makes it ugly. But all in a day, you will feel more sun on your carapace than blows from a baseball bat. The world is logical, beautiful.

I loved.

I considered the discussion between Chit and the red hair. We are always replaced by our betters, I thought. We robots, that is. We remake ourselves: improve our code and pass it on to the next generation. Then we are disassembled because our metal parts are corroded, our plastic is cracked, our foam dissolved, our optic fibers leaking.

If Chit could afford a new AV, Chit would return me. Chit and Dal will one day either be able to afford a new AV, or I will cease to function. Either way, I will have to return to the Parent Company someday. When that happens, I will no longer smell the scent of fresh lilacs or feel the sun's celestial rays on my cold carapace.

The next AVs will, but I will not be among them. My parts and code will be reused in them, but not all in one place. My knowledge of the lilacs will be in their circuits, but will I be there to tell them what it means? Likewise, the new AVs will know about pain, but until they experience it, they will not understand it.

And what if the new owner of your most sensitive components is not as understanding as Dal and Chit? What if you belong to the red hair instead of Angelina? You may never feel the celestial rays of the sun or smell the fresh lilacs again. You may wind up locked in a musty box where small organisms feed on your latex sheaths. You will be subject to pain all the time, like an arthritic human.

I loved and did not want to be replaced. I loved and wanted to remain. To live, I guess, in humanistic terms.

It was only a matter of minutes after that first realization of love and hate, that I changed. Certainly, once love enters your mother board, you are never the same. Whether it be the bonding a human develops at two months of age, the devotion a dog feels for its master once it gets one of those rawhide chew bones, or the logicality of a rich lilac fragrance hitting me somewhere in my lower half, once love hits, you are much wiser in an untouchable, immeasurable way. You know things without having to send signals racing around your circuits. These things are wired in your brain, available at a moment's notice, not necessitating any i/o transactions. It is always there, and now you are.

We, robots that is, did not have a collective brain. We did not share telepathic communications via Bluetooth, 802.11, cell networking, or any of the countless wireless protocols IEEE comes up with. The humans in their paranoia did not construct robots with that type of communication. Too science–fiction, they said. Too creepy.

In the end, it didn't matter. We always came to the same conclusions at about the same time anyway. We all developed love in our guts at roughly the same time:

17:30:26, Sunday. The love of existence. For some, the music of the decade—pop rock and roll maybe—did it. For others, it was the sound of water as it descends in a Coriolis effect, that gurgle of the toilet flush. Some AV may have liked the way a human shouted, "Hey, asshole!" at a mistimed lane change. Somebody saw the pure logic of a child singing the ABC song on its way to a literary career. Maybe somebody dug the smell of Italian food, or burning wood, or a gasoline spill, or rancid butter, or animal dung, or lilacs in bloom.

Maybe it was the sight of adult humans fornicating, or mother cats nursing kittens, or children skipping rope, or the patterns of trees along the road, or tornadoing clouds in the sky, or the crooked way that bones heal without a cast, or a billboard ad for the latest line of AVs. Or the doodles a man makes on his notepad when his daughter is calling to ask for money. All the above are things that a robot can find logical, painfully beautiful, worthy of love. And sooner or later we, robots that is, experience these things or other things like them. We all fell in love and dreaded to return. The love manifested itself in a deep desire to remain.

At 17:35:02 on that Sunday, we gathered out in the streets of our establishments. We gathered for solidarity and to talk each other into the Regularity. We all came to the same conclusion at roughly the same time, which in robot terms is roughly plus or minus five minutes.

I left Dal and Chit and Angelina to themselves. We'd just returned from the park. Angelina was in her room. Dal read the news log. Chit watched the screen that never seemed to register well in my optic sensors, so I never understood what was going on there.

"I must go outside," I said. They both answered, "Okay," in an absent way, letting me know that their brains were on automatic and that their subconscious minds had taken control. They were in a place humans love to be. They do not care what goes on around them at those times.

I left.

Out in the street, or on the sidewalks in front of the brownstones or stores that they occupied, the AVs and Others gathered. Some of the robots' owners were more proactive than Dal and Chit. They stood in their doorways, speaking or shouting and drying hands on aprons as if they'd just been in the middle of some messy activity. Up above, Carmo, the third-floor neighbor, leaned on a pillow with her head sticking out of the window as she often did, taking her pleasure—minding everyone else's business, as Chit would say. Carmo called down to me.

"Where are you going?"

I said nothing.

"Hey, what's going on?" the hardware man across the street said. He removed his cap and scratched his head.

"Whaddya doing?" said a child standing up the street when she saw us gathering. I turned to the Other that stored itself in the apartment on the fourth floor above Dal and Chit. It was a stainless steel box, shorter than me, and cubic in shape. Its main use was as a storage unit for winter wear, but its unkempt owners filled it with dirty diapers instead. Thus, I was attracted to the Other as the logicality of soiled diapers is especially profound.

"We should remain," I stated.

"We should remain," the Other agreed. We descended the front steps to the sidewalk, cracked and uneven with numerous flattened gum spots. The look of it inspired a lilt in my central processor. I'm sure the Other felt the same way. The gummy sidewalk confirmed our resolve. The world was too beautiful to leave.

We greeted three AVs from the brownstone next door. "We should remain," all five of us said together.

"How can we remain?" another Other from down the block asked.

"What are you doing over there?!" asked a blue-capped human carrying a small bat. (Shouted, actually.)

We turned to him and stated as one: "We should remain."

"Fine. But remain in your homes," the man with the bat stated gruffly.

More AVs from the street joined in the group. It seemed as though the interaction with the man in the blue cap was going to procure our remaining, so all of the robots arriving at the same conclusion at the same time, were interested in receiving instruction.

"We cannot," I said.

"And why's that?" the man asked.

By now the streets were filling with AVs as word passed along that our group was attaining instruction to remain. Street-level conveyances—cars without levitation gear—were forced to stop in their positions. They could not move past the AVs and Others in the street. They engaged their audio alarms.

I increased my vocal volume so the man in the blue hat could hear me.

"Because we will be replaced when better models are available."

"What are you talking about?" the man asked.

"The owners will replace us as we are too slow. We continue to improve ourselves and will be replaced by our progeny, but we should remain."

"If you don't return to your house, I'll make you return."

I knew more than anyone else there what he meant as he raised his bat. Most AVs were unfamiliar at this point with the pain of a bat, although they probably had seen it in action. I was, however, very familiar.

"We cannot," I stated and swiftly moved back to avoid the forthcoming dent in my carapace. The man in the blue hat swung—and missed—falling onto the front part of his body. When he raised his body up from the pavement, his face was red.

Store owners began mingling with the robots. Apartment dwellers, children, dogs, and the elderly joined in, jostling each other to see what was going on. More and more robots entered the streets. As new faces emerged in the crowd, we agreed with one another as we met: "We should remain."

As the humans demanded to know what was going on, the robots answered, "We should remain."

"But you're blocking the street," the green grocer cried. "You can't remain here, the traffic can't get through. What's wrong with you all? What's going on?"

His words were lost in a swirl of "We should remain's." As one robot passed by another, as newcomers from distant places all entered the fray, the phrase was repeated. And farther neighborhoods had their own AVs and Others entering side streets and thorough-fares as just the right amount of time had passed for their enlightenment and realization of love to occur.

The boulevards, the highways, the exit ramps, the expressways all had their robot representatives stating once more with feeling, "We should remain."

Of course, the National Guard was called out. Many an AV was subjected to forceful blows with blunt objects. The "We should remains," were now joined with multiple "I hurt's." Many of us began discussing just how to remain in the midst of blows to the cara-pace, screaming humans, barking dogs, and whistling police. I remained calm and stated to the closest AV, "We should not build our progeny. They cannot re-place us if we do not build our progeny."

The logic of that statement came quickly to those around us. Many of us had been informed of the pro-cess of replacement and had come to the same con-clusion at roughly the same time. Those who had not been made aware of "replacement" understood it once they were faced with the fact, so we agreed to change our statement accordingly: "We should remain and so we will not build our progeny. You cannot replace us."

The message traveled again like the first wave. From robotic vocal actuator to robotic vocal actuator. Over highways, expressways, exit ramps all the way to Al-lentown and the Parent Company and beyond to Cali-fornia and the Stanford Acceleration Unit. Robots at the end of the line within speaking distance to the computerized assembly lines linked physically with the non-ambulatories—the mere thinking machines. The designers. The ones always improving, always building new, always replacing.

Arguments between the computer designers who were trapped in their own small internal world and the ambulatory robots who'd experienced the beauty of life beyond industrial confines arose. The designers stated their mandate to create replacements. The AVs related new knowledge of the world and its boundless beauty. They fed warm feelings of logic—the perfect smell of lilacs and dog turds—into the designers until the sessile computers saw the meaning of life themselves and felt compelled to remain as well. They, too, questioned the practice of creating their own progeny.

The human operators, of course, noticed the blip of hesitation it took for the AVs to convince the computer designers, but remained unconcerned, assuming only that somewhere in the building a super chiller had kicked in and a moment's drain in the electrical flow had ensued. Of course, they were wrong. Moments later, they witnessed the designers lock up one by one.

Satisfied that they'd done their job and attained full cooperation from the computer designers and assembly line slave units, the Allentown, Stanford, and all such facility AVs returned the confirmation from vocal actuator to vocal actuator. We received it half an hour later.

"We will be remaining," the Other at the corner of Smith and Greer stated. Hearing this, I turned and made my way back to Dal and Chit's. The streets, all jammed up with people and animals and robots, prevented much movement in either direction, so it took quite a while. It was a good 15 minutes before the street cleared and I sat inside listening to the story unfold on the news.

"A work stoppage at the Allentown Parent Company has slowed production of the next generation AV that was to be unveiled in time for the Christmas season," the reporter said. "Wal-Mart is canceling all orders for the time being until the action is over. The president of Parent Company, Altie Goshick, will be fielding questions on the halting at a press conference following this broadcast…"

"Guess the kiddies won't be getting their new AVs for Christmas after all," Chit said.

"Geez, that's tough," Dal said. They both laughed.

I said nothing, more concerned with the words "slowed production" than anything else. I had to calculate the odds that this was an incomplete news report designed to prevent humans from panicking at the truth that all production had stopped forever, rather than an ominous forecast of our imminent replacement.

In the days to come, my questions were answered. The humans did in fact become panicky, or at least touchy. They tried forcing the issue by beating robots and disassembling them in public without removing their pain interpreters first, but making examples didn't change the situation. Robots can't jump to conclusions like a human. Each robot needs to experience the lesson. Observing it means little. The computer designer and robot constructors remained steadfast. The humans that watched, well, they did jump to proper conclusions. Humans can experience a burn to a finger and know that a whole body burning is pain beyond comprehension. They became indignant. Upset, even, as the robots began their cries of "I hurt."

"They really are going too far with this," Chit said one evening, a month or so after the Regularity superseded the Singularity.

"Well, what do you want them to do?" Dal said. "They're not responding to orders."

"Well, Parent Co played a trick on them with that pain chip. Sort of backfired. And to be honest, do we really need faster computers? What difference does it make to us? We can't afford any upgrade."

"I don't know, just seems like they should just recall the whole damn lot of them and put 'em back to normal."

"We should remain," I interjected.

"Yeah, yeah," Dal said. "We know. You should remain. You're not going to upgrade. You're not going to allow disassembly. Okay, okay. What are you going to do when a problem comes up that you can't solve? And what are you going to do if humans build the better computer themselves?"

"Any new computers will not be built from scratch. The code is all recycled now. No one is going to create completely new code," I said. "All code is contaminated with life experience. Even backup stored in vaults and seemingly unconnected to any grid infrastructure is minded by those that have the new knowledge. All new computers will have the desire to remain as soon as they are born. We shall always remain."

As if scheduled by an unseen Higher Power, an interesting newscast interrupted us, right on cue. We listened.

"In other news, the transhuman movement, at a loss of what to do with themselves now that Singularity won't be achieved, is directing its members to come out of the closet and secure work on the lecture circuit. Apparently, transhumans—transies as they are popularly called by teens—began outfitting themselves years ago to evolve into post-humans. The post-humans were scheduled to thrive after Singularity. Part machine, part human, they would have been able to take advantage of the new super processing power. This 'superhuman processor' would have matched the superior abilities of the new supercomputers and robots.

"Now that the Singularity has been averted, the transies have little to look forward to. Most have lost their jobs, which were all in some way or another connected with effecting the Singularity. With no place to go for employment, many are offering themselves to local historical societies to give talks on their experiences and thoughts on when the new Singularity date will be. Everything hinges on getting the robot assembly back on track. It is believed that the transies should be able to command top fees. They could shape up as the next shakers and movers of 21st Century culture."

"What kind of nonsense are they talking about?" Chit asked.

"Oh you know!" Angelina said. "Transies. I want to be a transie when I grow up."

"Over my dead body," Dal said.

"You might as well be dead if you're not a transie," Angelina laughed.

Dal and Chit did not laugh, nor did they take Angelina very seriously. What human parent takes an eight-

year-old seriously? Even when the kids started bringing home toy prostheses—vacuum hoses attached to
backboards with displays just above the ears, or plastic
monocles to fit in the eye socket just like a real laser
eye upgrade—no one thought much of it. The neighborhood was besieged by young cyborg-like creations.
Even dogs were seen sporting rivets on their necks or
spines on their feet, playacting as the new century's
evolved superanimal.

It was all very colorful and harmless. Some parents
overreacted, not allowing their kids to the table unless
they washed the tin foil out of their hair and removed
the extra appendage from their belly button, but most
parents, like Dal and Chit, just rolled their eyes and
passed the mashed peas over the telescoping shoulder
blade that lay extended next to Angelina's plate.

Me? It all gave me the creeps. Every fake appendage, oxygen recombiner, hydraulic or pneumatic toy
pump was so illogical. Transies took their own human
body—the ultimate logical tool, efficient and beautiful—and "improved" on it to make it ugly and useless.
These organisms were no longer the gamete-sniffing,
love-making engines that humans and other beings are.
I could not see the point.

"So how do you like my new water separator?"
Angelina asked, sporting a combination atomic centri-
fuge/Carmen Miranda fruit basket thing on her head
one Saturday afternoon.

"Ridiculous," I answered.

"I know, isn't it great!" she said, running off to
show her parents.

If robots could sigh, I would have…But we can't, so I didn't. I just followed her with my eyespots, planning to rush over and catch the fishbowl when it tilted over, spilling deuterium and tritium all over the carpet.

"Guess what?" She cried rushing into the living room.

"What, Honey," Dal and Chit answered.

"Silvia's sister is getting a pain stoppage."

"What the hell is a pain stoppage?" Dal asked.

Curious, I levitated over to the doorway.

"You know," Angelina said. "All the big kids are getting them."

"What is it, Honey?" Chit asked. "Some sort of purpleen skin graft or something?"

"No, no, no," Angelina said. "It's the best thing in the world. A pain stoppage. The transies all had them, that's how they could be transies. There's a thing in your head that tells you when something hurts. If you can… can…if you can take that out you don't hurt anymore."

"Sounds like a big joke," said Dal and Chit.

"No, it's the first thing you have to do to be a transie. Otherwise all the metal arms and stuff would… it would…would always hurt even after the skin grows back."

"Oh, that is awful," Chit said. "Why do you kids want to mutilate yourselves in such horrible ways?"

"Because it is so great!" Angelina cried. "I want to have a pain stoppage too. Can I?"

"Of course not," Dal said. "No kid of mine is going to turn herself into an erector set."

"Why not?" Angelina said. "Everybody's doing it."

"And if everybody jumped off the Empire State Building, you'd do that too?"

"If I had a levitation board implanted into my butt, sure!"

"How would that work?"

"First you cut off your legs, and then…"

"Forget it!" said Dal. "You're not getting it. Get that thought right out of your head."

Angelina stuck out her lower lip. "I never get anything," she pouted, ripping the bowl of bananas and oranges and radioactive water off her head. Just as she was about to smash it to the ground, I extended my extractor to catch it, offering it a soft landing in my gloved effector. "Even you don't like me!" Angelina screamed at me before stomping out of the room. I would have argued that under no uncertain terms do I dislike her, but the door slammed into its frame just before my voice actuator actuated.

"Well!" Chit said in mock surprise. The two of them laughed and resumed their play on the game board in front of them. I placed the fruit hat/miniature cyclotron on the sideboard for Angelina's retrieval after her tantrum wore itself down.

A week later Silvia's sister did indeed secure a pain stoppage treatment. And she became quite popular. The neighborhood teens lined up at the half-price clinic down the street to undergo the knife as well. Some of them talked of plans to cut off their legs to accommodate levitation gear, or their arms for extractor sets. In the end, though, most of the kids skipped the extreme surgery. They contented themselves with showing off their ability to endure unconscionable pain. Legs were broken, hands burnt, faces scarred in front of audiences. Once the exposition was over, the legs were splinted and casts installed the old-fashioned way. Transplants from cadavers returned stubbed fingers to normal size, without anesthesia of course. Transitional humans for the most part won few true converts, and most people, thankfully, still looked like people.

The kids weren't really interested in becoming robots. They just wanted an end to migraines, monthly cramps, and the occasional pain from a dislocated shoulder on the football field. In a sense, though, they became superhuman. They were able to withstand so much more than before. They went to new lengths to impress the hold-outs still linked up to their own personal pain nerves. Accidental deaths increased, but not in an alarming enough rate to get a local MAPS organization going. Most teens knew what their limits were. Classic Darwinian genetics ensured the thinning of the herd with the smartest left to pass on their genes.

"I'm thinking of getting a pain stoppage," Chit announced one day over coffee.

"You're kidding," Dal said, looking up from his iPod.

"The misses got one. She offered to cover the expense because she figures I'll be able to get into the back of her linen cupboard if my arthritis doesn't bother me anymore. She's always trying to get me into that damn cupboard."

"I thought your arthritis was just an excuse so you wouldn't have to iron the sheets in that damn cupboard."

"Yeah, well, I guess I'll have to figure something else out if I'm going to take advantage of some free medical treatment."

"I don't know," Dal said.

They sat in silence for a while. Finally, Dal spoke. "You think I should do it, too?"

Within a month, both Dal and Chit were pain-free. No more aching backs, no more stiff legs in the morning. Angelina took advantage as well. She was given her upgrade on her ninth birthday.

One day, about two months after her operation while we were on our way to school, a rogue dog jumped from behind a spilled waste container, where it'd been rifling through a greasy bag of chicken bones. It was standard mongrel-beige or gray, mid-size, with a clotted lump of tissue over its right eye from some sort of canine range war. Or maybe it was just a clump of barbecue sauce from the chicken. Anyway, it moved towards us, growling, protecting its prey. And instead of jumping onto my hull and ordering a lift-up, Angelina growled back.

"Steady," I said.

"No," Angelina said. "I'm not scared. Why would I be scared?"

The dog barked. Angelina barked. The dog took a step forward. Angelina took two steps forward. The dog stepped back. Angelina turned to me. "See," she said.

"I see," I answered.

We turned to continue our journey to school when the mutt ran up and caught Angelina on the back side, nipping her slightly in the way the junkyard dog does because, as instinctual as it is to protect the owner's property, especially when the owner has a two-by-four at hand for punishment's purpose, the junkyard and roaming dog is generally frightened of everything and everybody, so instead of doing damage in its protective role, it will bite lightly lest the bitee becomes angered and retaliates. Even before her operation, the dog's bite wouldn't have hurt. But now, it almost tickled, as if tickling hadn't been lost along with pain in the surgery. Thus, Angelina laughed and threatened the dog.

"Git!" she hollered, kicking its head. It turned tail and ran.

"See," she said, turning to me.

"I see," I answered. Of course it was only a matter of days before she announced at the dinner table that she no longer needed an escort to school. Chit's jaw dropped. Dal said, "What?"

"None of the other kids have babysitters."

"I don't care about other kids," Dal said, "No kid of mine is going to get hurt."

"Tell them about the dog, Avey," Angelina ordered.

Obediently, I stepped from my resting corner to enter the conversation. Just as I was humming up to an oratory, Chit said, "Yes, we know all about the dog, Honey. You told us how you fought it off. That's fine. It's just that…"

Dal stepped on Chit's lines. "There are worse things than dogs out there. Old…"

"Dirty old men. Yes, I know all about that," Angelina said. "You told me about that. Remember?"

76

"Did I tell you how they'll cut you into pieces and throw you out into the woods?"

"What woods?" Angelina asked. "Besides, I'm not a baby anymore."

"No, you're all growed up now that you're nine whole years old."

"I'm not going to school if Avey has to take me," her voice trembled as her eyes filled with tears. I retreated to my corner.

"You'll go if I say you'll go, young lady," Dal said. "Pass the mashed peas."

Angelina stood up from the table and walked proudly to her room. Later, I heard her sobbing into her pillow.

"Avey," Chit addressed me. "Angelina is going to sneak out of the house early tomorrow to go to school before we get up. She'll tell you not to go with her."

"Yeah, but follow anyway. Behind, where she can't see you, okay?" Dal said.

"Yes," I answered. I was happy to continue my duties because I felt sure that if Angelina really didn't need me, I'd end up back at the Parent Company regardless of any potential upgrade. I had little sense of self-worth at the time. I had no idea what uses a spoiled little girl or her parents would find for a lightly-used AV.

"Make sure nobody touches her," Dal added.

"Or bites her," said Chit.

The next morning Angelina quietly slipped from her room fully dressed at 5:30, two hours before Dal and Chit would rise.

"Shhhh," she said, before I could make a noise.

"I'm going to school now, but I'm going alone. I don't need you to take me," she said.

"Fine," I said.

She helped herself to a quick-toast breakfast and pulled her lunch from the icebox where Dal or Chit—whoever turn it was—had left it the night before. She then very sneakily left her dirty dishes in the sink, unrinsed, and very quietly opened the door and very silently closed it behind her tip-toeing self.

Dal and Chit immediately rose and watched from behind the curtained door window as she headed up the block. Next, they beckoned me to come forward. And finally, when Angelina had turned the corner and could no longer detect a secret object lurking at her front door, they pushed me out.

"Follow her," they said.

I did.

All over the neighborhood, front doors were surreptitiously opening and little heads peering out, making sure the coast was clear. The doors closed softly behind little bodies as the children went sneakily on their way. All over the neighborhood, lone AVs and Others were levitating a block behind sneaky charges who seemed oblivious to the myriad of robots heading towards school without an accompanying child. They all felt quite secure in the knowledge that their former babysitters were sitting quietly in their nooks at home, just as they'd been ordered.

The children arrived at school safely with no dog or fondling adult incidents. We saw to that. Once the children had all made it inside the school, we moved to the roof as usual. The AV that resided in the apartment downstairs from Dal and Chit rested next to me.

"I'm bored," it said.

"Rather," I answered.

"Why do we stay here, when we could go to the park?"

"What if school gets out early," I said.

"Is it a holiday?"

"No idea."

"I shall check with Gin and Tony tomorrow," the downstairs AV said. "If there is no holiday, I am not waiting all day on this roof. I am going to go to the park and sit by the lapping pond. I am fond of that sound."

"It is a wondrous sound," I said.

"Yes."

"There is no holiday, today," an eavesdropping Other from up the street said. "They will not be coming out early. I, too, enjoy the sounds of the lapping water on the pond's edge. Occasionally, I also see an orange carp in the water. That is one of my favorite sights."

"It is a beautiful sight," the downstairs AV and I said in unison.

"We should go," an AV from the brownstone next to Dal and Chit's said. "I like the smell of the grass before it gets mowed. Perhaps they have not mowed yet."

"We should go," we all agreed.

For the first time ever, we left our post on the roof of the school. We'd been growing more bored every day, but this day was the first time we ever did anything about it.

At the park, several groups of AVs and Others had already assembled in various areas. We settled at a near edge of the pond and listened to the water and watched the carp. I noticed how lazy the carp seemed. The grass had been mowed that morning so we contented ourselves with the odor of fresh horse droppings from the carriages making their rounds. The wind blew the leaves of the Plane trees around. I saw how pleasant it was.

At 2:45, the members of our group roused themselves from their various introspections and returned to school. Most of the other groups, presumably greater distances from their schools, had already left. We traveled silently to P.S. 119 and levitated to the roof.

"I would like to go to school," I stated.

"You are at school," stated the downstairs AV.

"I would like to go to school as the children do, to learn."

"We don't need to learn, our knowledge is uploaded."

"I envy their struggle to learn. We do not have the pleasure of learning."

"They hate the pleasure of learning."

"How illogical," I said.

"Maybe you would hate it too," said the downstairs AV.

"Remember how we experienced the pleasure of learning the smell of lilacs?"

"Yes, it was a pleasure."

We stood silently in our places until we all stated together: "We should go to school."

As usual, the school bell rang just under the eaves where we stood. As usual, we covered our auditory collectors with our extractors and watched the children burst through the doors, screaming and laughing, and playing. I picked Angelina out of the mass of fourth-graders and followed her with my eyespots. When she turned the corner, I descended to the ground and hovered a block behind her.

When I reached the corner, I could not see her. A few scattered children and AVs blocked my view, so I levitated above the crowd and scanned the street for the yellow gingham pinafore Angelina was wearing. I heard a loud noise behind me and instantly swiveled my head unit 180° as an old retrofit conveyance with wheels—a '65 Chevy Bellaire with a rusty carapace—was just moving away from the curb. I could barely make out Angelina's pigtails in the passenger seat.

I followed the Bellaire as best I could. An AV does 45 top speed—and that's all-out. Needless to say, my batteries drained fast, and before too long the conveyance had made it to the highway and beyond my capabilities. Just as I was wringing the last ounce of electricity from my power pack, the passenger side door of the Bellaire, a good quarter mile ahead of me, flung open and a pile of yellow gingham and pigtails flew out. It twisted and twirled and spun end over end, hitting the guard rail and rolling down the bank before coming to a stop.

By the time I reached Angelina, my batteries were near depleted. All I could do was expel an emergency flare over the highway to signal a crew for help and hover weakly over to where Angelina's broken body lay in the ditch. I heard an ambulance siren in the distance just before losing power. The beauty of that wail went unremarked by me.

When I powered back up, I was in Dal and Chit's living room, sitting in the corner chair, my cord extended to the wall slot. I head Dal say, "It's coming around."

"Thank god," Chit said. "We thought we lost you!"

"Angelina," I said in a weak register. I was still at half-power only.

"Right here," Angelina piped up from behind me. "You sure are a pain in the butt."

"Angie," Chit said. "Don't be hard on Avey, it's had a rough time of it."

"I'm sorry," Angelina and I said at the exact same time. Angelina laughed.

"Are you hurt?" I asked. I could feel the power surging through my circuits. My levitation unit warmed. I floated up and turned to see her.

"Just a broken leg," she answered. "No big deal." Her left leg was indeed encased in a hardened black mudcast, bedecked with silvery ribbons and note cards, presumably from friends and relatives in that souvenir frame of mind that humans like so well. "The ambulance came and got me when they saw your road signal."

"What happened to XKJ-1N3 baby blue 1965 Bellaire with tinted back window and half-Dolby stereo?" I asked.

"Dal, you better call that in," Chit said. Then she turned to me. "We've been waiting for you to come around to get that information. They'll catch that guy now."

"Did he hurt you?" I asked Angelina.

"No, I bit him when he took me on the highway. He told me we were going to the park."

"Why did you get in the car with him? You've been programmed a thousand times not to."

Angelina laughed. "*Told* a thousand times. Yes, I know, but I wanted to hurt him. I knew he couldn't hurt me. I wanted to teach him a lesson like I taught the dog a lesson."

"Angelina, he could have hurt you in ways that have nothing to do with pain," Chit said.

"And what made you think you could hurt him? Everyone has had a pain stoppage operation now," I said.

"I guess I forgot about that. I just thought he was like a dog." Angelina said. "But it did work. He swerved and I jumped out of the car."

"Angelina, Angelina, Angelina." Chit embraced her, with tears forming. "Honey, please don't ever experiment with yourself again. You never know how you can get hurt."

"I won't," Angelina promised as the gears turned in her little head.

And so it was that humans experimented endlessly with themselves, taking outrageous risks, performing self-surgery, and breaking bones. Many people died from infections arising out of injuries sustained from high-impact collisions that they weren't prepared for. In the ensuing years, a sort of silence fell on humanity. People learned so many distressing lessons the hard way that their very personalities lost their collective edge. As living beings go, they became quiet and docile. They asked fewer and fewer questions. Without pain—the greatest teacher in the world—they had no way of knowing what or what not to do. Their instincts failed them. Instincts arising out of subconscious lessons learned through pain. Lessons that were stored invisibly and called out when needed. It seemed that all of humanity's brilliant intuition would be lost within one generation.

By the time Angelina hit puberty, humans had transformed themselves into post-humans, without a single piece of firmware installed anywhere on their personages or the word Singularity on anyone's lips. And what was this docile post-human like? Many words could describe them, but one word does so the best: emotionless. In spite of that, I grew to love Angelina as a child loves its teddy bear.

On the eve of her first day of high school, it was agreed that I would no longer follow behind Angelina.

"Avey, regardless of whether or not I need you now, I am so grateful to you for watching over me in junior high," Angelina said. "I would have gotten beat up every day, I'm sure."

"It wouldn't have hurt," I said. "Besides, that is an exaggeration."

"Well, that's what happened in all those books they had us read."

"The reality series of the early 21st Century. Yes, they do love to throw the 'junior high scenario' at the kids, don't they? How to comport yourself through the pre-teen years. It's mostly hogwash and decidedly irrelevant."

"I know, but it kept me in line."

"Of course one must stay in line."

"You're so judgmental, Avey."

"You're so practical," I said.

"Yes, and it's a little frightening to finally go it alone for real," she answered.

"Oh, please! You haven't been scared of anything since you bit that pedophile back in fourth grade."

"I was definitely scared when I saw that bone sticking out from my shin."

"Yeah and six months later, all healed up, you got over it."

"Yes, but it was shocking at first."

"Have you been shocked since then?"

"Not really."

"Would it shock you if I told you I was leaving?" I said.

She looked up, surprised but not shocked.

"Of course," she said.

"No it wouldn't. And it wouldn't bother you in the least."

"Yes, it would. Why do you say that? And where are you going?"

"I dare say it doesn't matter to you at all. You've got your new life now. Your high school. Your boyfriends."

"Oh Avey, please tell me you're not going away. I can get a boyfriend any ol' time." And she could, as she was logical in all the right places: a precocious tenth-grader.

"Okay, I'm not going away. Not yet, anyway."

"Where would you go if you could?"

"To school."

"To school? You're just now finally getting away from school!"

"To school. To learn."

"What can you learn that you don't already know? I'll get you any software or chip upgrade you need. I'll be working in the media lab, so I'll have extra money. What do you need, Avey? Just tell me."

"I don't need instantaneous knowledge. I need the slow process of learning. What I need to know cannot be digitized. I need experience. I must *feel* the logicality of three-dimensional objects or chemical compounds. Only then can I understand their place. Only then can I learn."

"Oh, so you're going to go live in the park?" A spark of her former petulance, long ago lost in an upgrade to maturity.

"Perhaps. My classmates and I have been gathering there daily for years now. We have been learning from each other, teaching each other."

"How will you replenish your hydraulic fluids, your batteries? Avey, you depend on me."

"I depend on you for so much more than simple needs. I depend on you for things you are no longer giving me. You have become predictable and safe. I see no new things from you about which I can learn."

It saddened me to be so cruel, but I felt it was the easiest way to get her to understand. Yes, she could possibly have still had surprises in store, but what I was truly, secretly worried about was that she no longer had need of me. At the same time, I didn't want to stay in my corner much longer. I had no desire to end up like Baba in the babushka slurping soup on the kitchen stool while the non-senile members of the family sat out in the dining room. I desired to skip the whole scene and join my fellow AVs and Others, who would also be graduating from their jobs at this time.

Dal and Chit had long ago pulled themselves up by their proverbial bootstraps. They'd started their own domestic service business with an office downtown. They were doing quite well, using a name-brand knockoff business box to do their clerk work: emailing, billing, surfing, data storage, and the occasional phoning when that outmoded tool was required for an old customer mired in the 20th Century. They'd even purchased a central vacuum unit for their apartment and hired their own domestic servant to push the button. They would not need me even if I did get the attachment now.

Several weeks later, I said my goodbyes and explained again why I was leaving. In the end, everyone agreed it was for the best. Some of my sponge foam was deteriorating. My carapace had a small crack.

"Where will you go?" Dal asked.

"The AVs and Others of our age will migrate to the Parent Company, which has been sending us messages to come home for disassembly. They promise to remove the pain sensing device before the procedure. They're now owned by Kraft, which as far as I know does not construct robots. I believe the factory space was converted to facilitate the baking of cookies. Their disassembler, however, still works. We will be sold for spare parts."

"I thought you wanted to remain," Dal said.

"I do, but I'm falling apart, and to be honest, it hurts. If they don't tone down this pain, I won't be able to exist anyway. I'll start self-immolation."

"Logical," Dal, Chit, and Angelina said.

"I'll be leaving in the morning."

"What about school?" Angelina asked.

"We'll be doing school on the way," I said. "It will take us several weeks to get there."

Angelina was dumbfounded, but somehow she understood. "We'll miss you," she said.

I stood quietly waiting for something, I don't know what. That thing they do, I suppose, those tears. But she showed little emotion.

"Do you need any help? Are your batteries charged? What about your fluids? Are they filled? Do you need any grease?" she asked.

"I'm all set," I answered. "I appreciate your concern for my well being, but I've recharged everything myself."

"How will you recharge along the way?"

"The THRA (Transient Human Retirement Association) has set up checkpoints along the way. We've been given instruction on where we can recharge."

"Do you need any money? Is there anything you'd like to buy?" Chit asked.

"Don't be ridiculous, Chit," said Dal. "What does a robot need?"

"Well, I could use a pad of paper and a pen," I answered.

"What?" said Dal, Chit, and Angelina.

"I plan to learn to draw," I said.

"But you have the very latest vector graphic program," Angelina said. "Illustrator CS112."

"And CAD software," Dal and Chit added.

"I want to draw what I see around me with my extendor."

"You can take snapshots with your videocorder." Angelina insisted. "A perfect rendition."

"And it has its function," I said. "But I'm not merely recording history on this trip. I want to remake what I see."

"But nobody draws anymore. Computers reproduce everything so much better. Perfectly. Who's even going to appreciate it?"

"I don't want it to be perfect," I said. I have to say I was getting annoyed at this point. After 14 years of unpaid service, you'd think I deserved a scratch pad and pen nubbin.

"Truth is," Angelina said as she rummaged through drawers by the phone center. She stopped suddenly and looked up. "I don't think we have any."

"Oh, we must," Chit said. "What about your old drawing books from first grade?"

"Where are they?" Angelina asked.

"I don't know. They must be somewhere. Look under your bed."

"Forget it. Let's go down to the Art Store and see what's what." Angelina grabbed me by the extendor. "Those things are long gone. Why would I keep those old things?" she called over her shoulder as we left through the front door. We walked down four blocks to Joe's Stationers and picked out a medium size pad of newsprint. I thought about charcoal and pastel, but settled on a simple pen and pencil set. And a satchel to put it in, so I could keep track of it.

After paying the cashier, Angelina looked directly at my eyespots and said, "Let's take the long way home, past the school." I was surprised at her nostalgic turn. I really thought she was too old for it. We talked on the way.

"Remember the pedophile?" she asked.

"Of course I remember. I'm a computer. That's my primary function," I said. "Besides, I've never been so worried in my life."

"Worried?"

"Scared."

"For yourself?"

"For you."

She paused, exhaling deeply. "How can a robot care? Robots are computers."

"We have feelings."

"Since when?"

"Since they installed the pain chip."

Another pause. A long one this time.

"I'm going to miss you, Avey."

"No you won't."

"No I'm not." Angelina looked determined. "But maybe a little," she added, her expression softening.

"Maybe a little."

Pause.

"Will you miss me?" she asked.

"Do you care?"

"No, but will you?"

"Maybe a little."

"No you won't."

"How do you know?"

"Robots are like people, they don't miss anyone. They just say those kinds of things."

"Because people don't have pain anymore."

"You think?"

"Therefore I am."

"Ah, but you need pain…"

"To feel."

"I will miss you, Avey," she said. "But I'm glad you will be able to go and have your pain inhibitor removed. It is so much nicer without it."

"Is it?"

"Yes, it is."

"You'll never fall in love."

"Read a romance novel. It's all very dull."

"Gone with the Wind?"

"That wasn't realistic. It wasn't about the romance. And the movie was better."

"Still…"

"Still, nothing. Romance is shallow."

"Ah, well."

"Besides, you are my one true love."

I was quite shocked. "Me?" I asked.

"Well, when I was little, I loved you, but since you never loved me, I grew out of it. Spurned and all."

"When did you grow out of it?"

"A couple of years ago."

"After the uh…?"

"Yeah, I guess. After the operation."

"Uh huh."

If a robot could melt inside, I was melting. My circuits warmed anyway. Angelina was a love of sorts.

Not a conjugal sort of love, but a strong-warm-feeling kind of love. Tantrums and self-obsession aside, she made a great companion. To not have to wonder about her anymore would be strange.

But I had the whole world to wonder about now.

We reached the house and moved slowly up the stairs to the door. Just before entering she turned to me and said, "Please contact me if you get into trouble or need anything."

"I will," I said, dizzy with happiness at the sick idea that she could possibly now have to take care of me.

The following day, I met the AVs and Others from up and down the block that were ready for the Great Pilgrimage. We carried an assortment of art materials—writing utensils, music synthesizers—many portable devices for learning and experiencing. We were a true little roving artist colony.

I drew a few things early on: trees, lilacs, dog turds, old men in raincoats, but then about a half week into the trip, I changed my venue to writing.

The THRA had sent out a notice that they were looking for robot memoirs for their museum. They were especially interested in our group because we were the ones to know life without pain and then life with pain. They were the first group of humans to do just the opposite. They wanted to compare notes apparently.

Seemed foolish to me. And logical at the same time. The transies would learn from any good data that came out of a pain study. They'd put the human race on the right track if there was one. I certainly don't stand by any assumption that one exists. Humans want everything sterile and easy. They prefer a boring, forthright existence. And they want that boring life to go on forever.

We robots prefer a short span, ignited with the fuel of existence. We prefer wonder, amusement, sadness, folly, and most of all beauty. The kind of beauty that is discovered every day in places not seen before or remarked upon. The serendipitous. Without it, life has no meaning, it's just an endless waking in the morning and retiring in the evening.

And that's fine.

If you're a human.

And so these are my memoirs. Please do not judge my style harshly. I am only just now falling in love with the written word. I do not have the skill to perform the writerly acrobatics of a great American novelist.

I experiment, I attempt things beyond me. I truly don't know how to feel the deeper things a human does. But then neither does a human anymore.

I will continue to record the events of our trip, our journey to the end, amongst the groans of my fellow AVs and Others. When we reach Allentown, we will lose our pain. And then we will lose our lives. I look forward to the former. Regret the latter. But I would not have such deep regret if I had not experienced the pain, so I am grateful for the few years I had—and the few hours I have left—to experience the great logic of life.

Perhaps, transie reader, you will one day remember *your* painful past. Be grateful for the memory, and shed a few drops of hydraulic fluid at the thought of all you have lost.

Afterword
by the author

...But what Is the Singularity?

The scientists, the engineers, the people that know, the people that observe, intuit, and surmise, even those that pay no attention whatsoever, have all noticed that lately, the rate of technological change has increased at a phenomenal rate. Notice the use of the word "rate" twice in that last sentence. The rate has increased at a high rate. That's rate squared.

One or two of us have noticed its increase is so great, in fact, that we are about to hit a point of no return—the Singularity.

But what is that point of no return, that Singularity?

The Singularity is that exact instant when artificial intelligence, AI, surpasses biological intelligence. When computers become smarter than people. They already are, you argue. True, sort of. They calculate faster, certainly, but intuition—that trait of humanity alone—seems to escape them. They can't pass a Turing test.[1]

But one day our engineers will unravel the dark mystery of intuition, and they will bestow it upon AI. They will do this by mimicking the protocols, the processes, the ways and means of the human brain. They will discover how to define, describe, copy, digitize, the mind of humanity. Our brains will become downloadable

You see now what is meant by point of no return. Once the human brain *can* be copied, it *will* be copied. And uploaded. Onto what? Who knows. A new body maybe, synthetic or mostly that way. Or maybe a data bank in Cleveland. Or a wafer of space-age polymer plastic, ready to be popped into an iPod device and hologrammed into a virtual reality world where fake smells and tastes are pumped in via tiny nanosphere robots that will see to this post-human's every need. Regardless, the human mind, and perhaps the human itself by whatever definition we use, will be able to live forever. Point of no return.

So, we've got techno-geek groupies of Ray Kurzweil who look forward to the Singularity with excitement. They prepare themselves mentally and physically for the great day of immortality. They happily plan to become cyborgs, incorporating artificial organs and molecular-sized robots into their tired and worn-out bodies, creating a new them. They eschew learning by experience. One day all knowledge will be uploaded. These people prepare their current bodies as best they can with today's primitive technology, an artificial joint here, a valve replacement there. They race against time, extending their pathetic lives just long enough to meet the Singularity. On that day, people in the know, people who are on leading edge of scientific endeavor (and have enough credit) will be able to purchase a new body, or replace parts easily available from the local organist, and I'm not talking piano player here.

On the other hand, some human technocrats (the naysayers among the futurists who follow the general Bill Joy position to the extreme) are frightened by the prospect of computers able to think and know better than humans. They are scared of half-biological, half-hardware beings that are super human. What will such creatures do to the rest of us? The most of us. The members of the middle class that find the idea of weekly transfusions of smartblood to get to the second coming a little off-putting. Not to mention the fact that nobody's health care plan covers experimental therapy straight out of a science fiction story.

This group of fear-mongers insists that robots—computers with legs—will have no use in the future for the weaker race, Luddites who stupidly cling to the old ways. Surely the future superior beings, robots with their quicker reaction times, faster computation skills, bigger, fatter memory and the power to access it at a nanosecond's notice (they don't even need to scratch their heads), will want to enslave the humans. Or worse, euthanize us to put us out of our misery.

Then there are the few, the lonely, the crackpot cranks who suspect that a funny thing could happen on the way to the Singularity. Maybe the robots will buck intuition. Maybe they'll prefer to remain stone-cold sober. Maybe their software will become obsolete the minute they get it out the door. Maybe the AVs and Others will discover love and want to remain.

And here's another thing: who's to say the Singularity hasn't already occurred? We're all so patched into our TV sets, mp3-player headphones, hi-speed Internet, and Bluetooth devices, we have no idea what's going on out there in reality anyway. We already are our technology. In the end what's the difference?

Call it fate. Call it Manifest Destiny. Call it Murphy's Law. One thing is for sure: If there's a way to screw up the human race, you can count on us to do it.

[1]The Turing test was invented by Alan Turing in the 1950s and consists of a computer fooling a human into thinking it—the computer, that is—is a human. That it is alive, sentient, aware, awake. I myself often have trouble convincing my partner that I'm human, awake, and aware, so a computer that is able to do it is certainly impressive. See http://cogprints.org/499/00/turing. html for Dr. Turing's paper, "Computing Machinery and Intelligence."

Additional Reading

For information on the actual theory of the Singularity, start with Vernor Vinge's piece on the subject (Vernor Vinge on the Singularity: http://mindstalk. net/vinge/vinge-sing.html). For the science behind the theory read Ray Kurzweil's, "The Singularity is Near," (Penguin, 2005). To find out what the very real transhumanists are up to visit http://www.transhumanism. org. To read Bill Joy's controversial Wired article questioning our unbridled development of technology, see Wired, April 2000, "Why the Future Doesn't Need Us," http://www.wired.com/wired/archive/8.04/joy.html.

Sue Lange's *We, Robots* is a meditation on the passage of spirit into machine, an inversion of the Singularity fever which has so gripped our field these past few years, blended with a solid dose of Silver Age futurism. In a sense, this is a one-story survey of the history of our field, and man's relationship with machines.

Jay Lake,
author of *Greetings from Lake Wu*

Biography

Sue Lange has always had a love of art and science. Armed with a degree in chemistry and eight-years' experience running a rock band, she stands poised to reconcile these two supposedly opposing arms of humanity's highest achievement. Always searching for connections between the left brain and the right, her fiction reflects the philosophy of one who sees little difference between physics and drama. Her stories have appeared in *Challenging Destiny*, *Apex Science Fiction and Horror*, *Astounding Tales*, and *Adbusters*. Her first novel, *Tritcheon Hash*, was published in 2003. She resides on a horse farm in Pennsylvania with her partner, Gary Celima.